Soul of the Storm

JEAN M. GRANT

ALSO BY JEAN M. GRANT

A Hundred Breaths
A Hundred Kisses
A Hundred Lies
Chasing Roses
Letters to Nobody
Seeker
Silent Creek
Will Rise from Ashes

Soul of the Storm

JEAN M. GRANT

Soul of the Storm

Book cover and scene break art by AK Westerman, AK Organic Abstracts | OA Graphic Design.

First edition, 2019

Digital ISBN 978-1-5092-2513-2

Second edition, 2026

Print ISBN   979-8-9923754-6-6

Digital ISBN 979-8-9923754-5-9

www.jeanmgrant.com

DEDICATION

To my sister Catherine, in loving memory.
A piece of my soul goes with you. With remembrance, my
heart heals.

One

A cheerful spring sun glared in Charlotte MacGregor's eyes. Instead of being a soothing welcome, the brightness aggravated an already pounding head. She pushed her discount sunglasses higher on the bridge of her nose then rummaged through her backpack to find her bottle of aspirin.

Her eyes burned from too much crying this week.

She called it pre-crying. Get it out of her system early, right? So, when *the day* arrived, her tear ducts would be empty.

Veronica had tried to convince her this trip to the Mad River Valley of the Green Mountains would be a chance to have fun during her high school students' April break, but Charlotte knew otherwise.

She leaned her head against the humming glass of the rear window in Veronica's sporty SUV, letting the vibration of tire against road battle the migraine.

Five years.

How had it been that long ago? The pain was a welt on her heart, a sore from yesterday.

So much could happen in five years...but in Charlotte's world, nothing good had happened. Instead of moving forward, she had fallen back. Back into old feelings. If only she could turn the clock back, too.

Veronica knew that her friend was in a crater-sized rut. That's why they were heading to Winterwood, Vermont for the week. To help Charlotte forget. To make her snap out of it.

There was no forgetting her sister, though. Did people think she *could* forget Julie?

She heaved a sigh laced with bitterness. With her pointer finger, she traced the infinity tattoo on the inside of her wrist, circling along faded black. The tattoo was over fifteen years old. She and Julie had gotten matching tattoos once they graduated high school. Irish twins some called them. Two peas in a pod. Throw any paired cliché at them. They had been inseparable.

She had once scheduled an appointment to have the tattoo removed but chickened out. Brands were meant to be reminders after all.

Lifting her head from the warm glass, she twisted the bottle cap, popped two aspirin, and sipped her now-cold vanilla latte she'd purchased at a rest stop on the Mass Pike.

"Chin up, Charlie girl. We're almost there," Veronica said from the front. She took a sharp turn, and Charlotte had to hold onto the door handle.

Oblivious to her lead foot, Veronica added, "We'll have a blast. Sunshine. Green."

More like mud and brown. Charlotte blinked away the returning tears. There were too many triggers today. Too much time on the drive from Boston with her wandering thoughts and in the front seats, gabbing, overly happy, touchy-feely Veronica and Josh. This whole third-wheel thing with her newlywed friends was a bad idea. At least she brought some work along. Maybe she'd find a bookstore.

"There it is. A sign for the Millstone Inn," Veronica said a few minutes later, her voice sickly sweet with excitement.

Oh, to find the joys in simple things. Did Charlotte find joy in anything anymore?

A good cup of coffee. She liked that. An engaging book. An afternoon nap. Comfortable shoes. An organized pantry.

Good grief, she aged herself fifty years.

Josh lifted his gaze from the map. "Terrific. My GPS stopped working, and this map is confusing. Who uses these things anymore when you have GPS? Hope we have Wi-Fi at the inn. That mountain pass was a dead zone."

Veronica pinched him. "Ouch! What the hell, Ronnie?" He plopped the map in a heap onto his lap, ignoring the folds.

"Josh, I'll take it." Charlotte shoved her hand between the front seats, and he deposited the tattered road map in her palm.

What Josh lacked in neatness and manners, he made up for in honesty and affection. He loved Veronica to the moon and back. He would never lie to her or treat her like dirt. He was a good one. There seemed to be so few of them these days.

Dating apps had been a disaster for Charlotte...and such a bad idea post-divorce. Maybe she was going to grow up to be like her spinster aunt Evelyn. Spinster? Even that word sounded like an old-lady word.

She snapped out of her melancholy and opened the Vermont map, lined up the folds, and refolded it properly. She tucked it into her red backpack, the one that still had new tags on it until this morning. The one that had been packed away into a box in her basement five years ago.

"A pity there's no snow to ski Sugarbush or Mad River Glen," Veronica said.

"Yah, unusually warm this year," Josh responded and added coyly, "What are we to do, Mrs. Meier?"

Veronica tossed her head back and giggled, her salon-perfect, strawberry-blonde curls bobbing.

Honeymooners. Charlotte rolled her eyes behind the sunglasses. Oh, how she remembered. The early days of fun and romance. Then came the fighting, the controlling, the cheating. She prayed her friends' marriage would last longer than hers had.

Why had she agreed to go on this trip with them? Thirty-somethings were too old for this party-of-three thing.

She drank the last drop of her coffee. She'd hold onto the cup to recycle at the inn.

They turned onto Main Street toward the Millstone Inn.

On the corner stood an outdoor sports outfitter. Charlotte's stomach churned, the coffee bitter on her throat, the taste of pain rising to join the sweet vanilla. She shied her eyes away, clinging to anyplace else. There, the post office. Nice and reliable. The toughest obstacles for postal carriers were barking dogs or lawn sprinklers. Or storms. Ugh. She withdrew her lip balm and applied it, the mint pleasantly tingling.

Trees lining the clean, trimmed streets of the quiescent town had yet to show their spring blooms. Their brown bark stood out stark against a sky-blue horizon.

A dazzling early April was a deceitful jester. New England was notorious for late snowstorms. Veronica and Josh had packed their skis despite the resorts being closed for the season. Josh said they might even climb up a mountain to ski down, but Charlotte knew Veronica didn't have that level of commitment in her. Veronica stuck to the easier ski slopes, usually green trails or the occasional blue, and then spent the rest of her time near the fireplace in the lodge. Josh was the daredevil though, skiing down double blacks.

Although they lived near Boston and received milder weather than the central hills near Worcester and the mountains of Vermont and New Hampshire, they had been pummeled with snow in January and February this year. Veronica had begged Charlotte to come along on a few trips north to slopes "like the good old days," but she declined. Her days of stepping foot on a mountain of any sort were long behind her. No more hiking, biking, or skiing. Flat land. City streets. Evenings in front of her television lesson-planning or watching mindless shows.

It might be April, but winter was never done until after Mother's Day. Her mom always waited until then to fill her planters. She loved pansies the most. Pansies were some of the first blooming annuals in spring. They tolerated the cold best.

They had been Julie's favorite flower.

Hardy and defiant, happy and bright, just like Julie.

Charlotte looked at the sky. She bet winter wasn't done with them yet. She shivered and zipped her fleece vest to her chin, despite the heat from the seventy-degree day.

Because of their crazy number of snow days at school, her students were behind, again, on their curriculum and projects. Toss in their February and April breaks, and she felt like summer would never arrive.

She needed this respite.

The principal was always understanding during this week and had allowed her to use extra personal days for this trip.

Veronica peered at Charlotte over her designer sunglasses. Adoring, crystal-blue eyes beheld hers. "We'll have a great week, hun. Ignore those meteorologists, too. Look! Spring is here. Remember, you chose this instead of Florida."

Charlotte forced a half smile in place of a grimace. Brown and gnarly and isolated instead of glistening sandy beaches filled with party people and slick, hot bodies. Brown and gnarly for the win. Isolation was the best part. It'd be easier to disappear here with a coffee and her students' reports and her training manual. She hoped her students were ready for the statewide testing coming up.

"Perhaps we can take a hike—" Josh began.

"No," Veronica said tersely.

He looked at her, puzzled.

She puckered her glossy pink lips, then said, "We'll find something else to do. Walk the town, explore the Mad River, eat loads of ice cream. I wonder if the inn has a firepit."

Josh didn't get it. The aching cleft in Charlotte's brain cracked farther down to her chest, right through her heart.

He pressed. "The hiking is fab. I thought we could—"

Veronica squeezed his knee.

"Ouch, Ronnie. My darling wife, we can't spend all our time in our room," he teased.

She laughed too quickly. "Oh, yes we could."

Charlotte sighed. Josh was slow to put it together, but Ronnie's not-so-subtle reminders finally jogged his memory.

"Oh, ah, yeah. You do love shopping." He recovered his valor while clearing his throat. He ran a hand through his sandy blond hair.

Like a helpless fly drawn to honey, Charlotte angled her head to the west. The cloudless sky revealed nearby Lincoln Peak and Mount Ellen at the Sugarbush Resort. Their brown hills lacked snow, except for areas far on the top, near the ski runs. The rest had melted with the unseasonable warmth.

A storm could be on the horizon. A storm could rush in and suffocate the world and allow the mountain to swing its rocky fist with a blow of death for those unlucky souls caught upon the ridge.

She exhaled the negative thoughts. Veronica was right. She needed a break. If it snowed and the ski resorts reopened, the lovebirds would hit the slopes and leave her alone in her room. It would be perfect.

One week. She could do this. She had brought science reports to grade and lessons to prepare. She also had her emergency response manual to review for the big seminar she organized for their school district. That seminar was scheduled for May. Plenty of stuff to keep her mind occupied.

She would review the annual CPR training, first aid presentation, and crisis intervention notes. A glutton for punishment, she had taken on that effort a few years ago to lead the school district's emergency response training. Anything to keep busy. Anything to be prepared...if.

She also had her laptop, never traveling without it. Today could be the day that Esteban sent her more news.

Two

Matiu Christiansen trudged toward the inn, his calf-high gumboots caked in mud. The sun dipped in the afternoon sky. "Ah, cripes," he mumbled. Late. Again. Nate would be put out. They had a full roster of guests this week, with it being April vacation in Massachusetts. New Hampshire ran different school breaks, so the guest load was spread over two weeks.

The inn was at max occupancy which meant more work. Even if the weather sucked this time of year, people needed to get away. Many went to Florida, but some stuck around in New England.

He juggled his hectic schedule in his mind. He disliked leaving Reka with Mrs. Wakefield, yet again, but he knew the widow enjoyed the companionship of his German shepherd.

He chugged from his water bottle and moaned as he stretched his back and cracked his neck. If more reckless out-of-towners thought they could conquer Lincoln and Ellen in this weather, then he would be needed on the mountains with the search and rescue—SAR—team. The ski patrol was done for the season, so all rescues were left to the SAR crew.

Matiu was up to his calves in mucking for his US Forest Service job, it being mud season after all. Did people not read conditions before embarking on a trail? Apparently not. His obligation to rescue stranded trampers took away from his time cleaning trails. But people would be people. Heck, the thrill always lured him, too.

Knackered and reminded of the two young bros he pulled from the mud this morning, he didn't see the black SUV heading for him as he crossed Main. The screeching tires roused his senses, and he dodged it.

The driver honked, stopped, and the passenger window rolled down.

"Watch it, man! Don't need to wipe you off my car bumper," the man hollered, thick with a Boston accent. *Cah bumpa.* Matiu cringed.

The driver leaned across her rude passenger and said pleasantly, "You okay?"

He shrugged her question away, shaking. "Nah, yeah."

"Huh?"

He nodded and patted his chest to indicate he was fine. "Speed limit on Main Street is twenty-five miles per hour, ma'am."

"Oh, Josh, I'm a ma'am! That guy sounds like he's from Australia. I'm going to love it here. Told you," he heard her say as the car turned onto the inn's cobblestone parking area.

Try New Zealand, lady. Flatlanders were all the same.

He reached the rear door to the inn, dropped his gumboots outside, and swapped them for a pair of shoes he kept by the door. The kitchen was quiet since it was Wednesday, and they only served dinner Thursdays through Saturdays. Today was prep and experiment day. Nate gave him a half nod as Matiu entered. Reusable grocery bags overflowing with fresh produce and kitchen staples lined the counter.

"Let's try that new salmon recipe, Matiu. I have some ideas to spice up the béarnaise for tomorrow."

Matiu washed his hands, put on an apron, and set to work.

A light breeze whistled through wind chimes, and cars groaned down Main toward the lively crowd at Finnigan's as Matiu made his way home. The streetlights were his companion as he mentally reviewed tomorrow's schedule. He had a morning tour group to guide on a paddle of class one and two whitewater, an afternoon shift at Barrett's Bookstore, where he could leash Reka outside due to the nicer weather, before heading to the inn for his dinner shift. He was off mucking crew duty tomorrow at least.

Cripes, he did too much.

He crept up the stairs and dropped his muddy gumboots at his door, hoping to not rouse Nora Wakefield below.

Reka barked.

"Ah, cripes," he said to himself, shaking his head.

How could he forget his sweet gal?

"Matiu? That you?" Nora poked her head through her opened porch door, Reka clambering beside her in the door yard.

"Just me. Was tossing my boots upstairs first," he said and descended the stairs.

"How's my girl today, Reka? Helping Nora with her cooking?" He knelt to the German shepherd's level and allowed her to lick his face. She sniffed his fingers. "Salmon tonight, my sweet." He shook a bag beside him. He whispered, "With bacon…"

"She was well-behaved, like always."

He cleared his throat. "Thanks. I appreciate it this week. I'll bring her tomorrow for my evening shift at the inn. She'll be joining me on a tour and at the bookstore. I'll get to that yard work for you next weekend, if that's okay?"

She swatted him away and nudged her glasses up on her nose. "No rush. The street sweepers haven't come to collect the winter sand from the sidewalks and roads yet." She shivered, bundling tighter in her rose-colored sweater. "Winter's not finished, as much as those flat-landers think it is. Sure hope they brought snowshoes and not sandals."

He smiled politely and took Reka upstairs. "Cheers. See you tomorrow."

He unlocked his door, clicked on a light, and caught himself before tripping on his rescue gear and rucksack. He weaved past the pile, grabbed a soda from the fridge, and scooped a portion of the meal for Reka on a dish.

"Don't get used to it, sweet girl. It's just a treat. You need to eat your kibble to stay fit. I'm sure there will be people to help on the mountain this week." He exhaled.

"You're so patient with me," he whispered, scratching behind her ear. He strolled to the couch. It was early afternoon in New Zealand, so he dialed his cousin.

Jacob answered.

"Hey, mate. Your mum home?"

"Matiu! She's buggered. Just got home from her morning shift at the hospital. How's life?" Jacob's youthful voice came.

"The town's chocka this week. Spring break. Mud season. You'd love it. All good."

"When are you coming to visit again?"

Matiu's heart squeezed. "Soon, mate, soon. Put your mum on?"

He heard rustling as his cousin Kura snatched the phone from her son. "Matiu," she breathed into the phone with delight, but Matiu deciphered the exhaustion in it. "How are you?"

"All good. You?"

"It's bloody cold today, but otherwise all good," she said.

"You're still working morning shifts at the hospital? Thought the doctor ordered you to rest?" He rubbed his knuckles on his grimy jeans and sipped the soda.

"I need to make ends meet."

"I've almost got the money saved, Kura. I'll be home soon. I'll see you right."

She sighed heavily into the earpiece. "I'm no bludger. I can't take your money."

"I reckon you can, and you will. Let me help, cuz. Plus, I could watch Jacob and stuff. He can help me at my outfitter."

"He has school, and you'll be too busy with setting up the business." She coughed. "You never take no for an answer."

"Nope."

She chuckled. "How's your mum?"

"Good. Keeping busy with her work at the university. She's been looking into openings in history departments in Wellington. She's keen on the idea of moving back home with me," he said, trying for a light attitude. "I miss her."

His mom lived in California, which felt so far away these days.

Reka advanced and curled at his feet. She heaved a heavy sigh, her breath warm on his calf.

They talked about little things, avoiding conversation about weighty subjects. Soon enough he'd return home to Aotearoa, to New Zealand. His skin itched with the desire to be among his maternal family. His move back home was only a few months away. He'd finish this upcoming summer season, and he'd have enough in the bank for the outfitter he dreamed of opening near Queenstown.

He'd been saving for five years. With the right loan, he could make it work.

Even though Kura had access to governmental aid, he needed to *be* with her. He'd read about new multiple sclerosis treatments she could try. She needed an honest bloke in her life. Jacob needed a respectable role model. Mum coming home with him would be a bonus.

It would all work out.

Once he disconnected with Kura, he lifted the business plan binder from the messy pile on his cluttered coffee table. He pushed this morning's half-full tea mug aside and thumbed through the pages of possible business locations with reasonable leases. The plan was set. All he needed was the place. Some mates back home were willing to jump at the opportunity. Kura had been speaking with investors. All he had to do was to pinpoint the finance group for his business loan.

He cast a look at the framed photo above his small TV. Aoraki stood majestic...and ready. His father had taken him on many of the tracks in the valley, on the glaciers, and around the mountain before they moved to the states. Sure, Vermont and New England owned their share of 4,000-footers, but nothing compared to that alpine glory in his homeland.

"Oh, you'd love it, sweet girl," he said to Reka. Her ears perked, and she tapped her tail.

Soon. First, he needed to get through these two busy weeks. No distractions. Punch the clock, do his jobs—cripes, so many jobs—and crash on his couch alone each night. That was all he had in mind. Perhaps catch up on some sleep and get a morning run with Reka.

He pulled on his quilt, reclined, and let his dead-tired body rest.

Three

Charlotte expected the knock at her door. She sighed, closed her laptop, and opened the heavy oak door to find Veronica standing there. "Yeah?"

"Did you not see my texts? We're going to tour the town. Come with us," Veronica pleaded, her voice hinging on annoying.

"I've got papers to grade and my presentation to prepare. I'll come later," Charlotte half lied. She had already tackled part of the stack last night after they arrived and would easily be done this afternoon. The lesson planning could be done by tomorrow. The presentation was mostly set; she'd just update the previous year's slide set.

Veronica chewed her lip, feigning exasperation. "Well, I made reservations for tonight, okay?"

"Sure," Charlotte relented.

Her friend paused. She tapped a finely manicured nail on the door jamb. "Charlie, look. I brought you here to get fresh air." She gave an exaggerated chin flick toward the laptop. "Are you actually grading papers?"

Charlotte thinned her lips. No *more tears, no more tears.* Julie would not have had it. "There's no Wi-Fi in the room, and my phone is spotty. The mountain is blocking good cell reception. So, no, I'm not gloom scrolling, or checking emails, or anything. Stuff is loading at a snail's pace. If I did want to go online, I need to use the media area where the connection is better. So, no, I'm not online. I *am* doing work."

Veronica leaned in and embraced her, her perfume nearly migraine-inducing. "This weather is amazing. Perhaps we can hit a trail or two? See flowers or something? Here, in town. Not in the mountains. They call us flatlanders. We'll stick to flat land. You love flowers."

"It's too early for much of anything. Everything is in planters. The daffodils aren't even blooming."

Josh appeared at Veronica's side. He scratched his head, ruffling his wayward hair. "We'll bring you a coffee from the café?" he offered.

"Sure."

"Dinner?" Veronica pushed.

"Okay." Charlotte nodded and wriggled from her friend's tight hold. She closed the door but overheard their frustrated, lowered voices. Old inn, thin walls. Veronica sort of got it. She knew. She tried. Everyone tried.

The stack of science research papers beckoned her. On the top was Kesha's paper on "The Effect of Pollution on Bioluminescent Bacteria." Below it, she had to chuckle at Robert's: "The Fate of Storm Chasers." His work was always an animated, amusing read. She wouldn't be surprised if that bright student in her tenth-grade class ended up an actual tornado chaser. He loved nature, meteorology, and the thrill of the chase. He reminded her of a younger Julie.

She sighed, put his paper aside, and dug into Kesha's with her handy red pen.

A few hours later, with a kink in her neck from sitting in the 1950s-era armchair and tired of correcting grammar on top of scientific reasoning and evidence, she replaced a paper on the stack and rose.

Where was that coffee?

This rustic inn didn't have a coffee pot or Keurig in the room, and she'd already skipped the offered breakfast. That meant she had to go somewhere. Veronica had probably dragged Josh into every shop from here to Waterbury.

Too morose yesterday, she had yet to unpack. That would kill time. Although her vacation was only for six days, she decided to put her clothes in the antique white dresser. She opened a drawer with eye-catching detail on the rose-embellished knob. She inhaled cedar, admiring the dovetail corners.

Fragrant rose potpourri sat in a porcelain dish on the dresser. Veronica had fine taste with locales. The inn was quiet despite being booked solid.

She neatly put away her clothes. She had overpacked as usual, but she never knew what to expect with New England weather. It might be balmy one day and blustery the next in early spring. There could be snow on the mountains and sunshine in the valley.

She removed her camera bag from the backpack and placed it on the dresser. Then she made her way to the pedestal sink in the bathroom. She placed her assorted toiletries on the ledge below the oval mirror, lining up each by order of use, saving her sleep aid for last. She re-frained from looking in the mirror at the dark, half circles that certainly cradled her eyes. Cry hangovers sucked. Her olive complexion made the aftereffect worse. Con-cealer didn't help.

When they checked in yesterday, the owner hinted at the inn's ghost stories and encouraged them to join others in the Millstone Inn's dining room for dinner to hear more tonight. Guests had priority seating, but it was by reservation only. Last night, she was relieved to eat in her room, happy with a granola bar, too familiar with her own ghosts.

She yawned and peeked out her large window, which offered a view of the town hall and offices. At least she faced away from the mountains. The old inn rested at the top of a hill with amazing vantage points. Veronica and Josh had gotten a room with a view of the mountains. She'd already noticed the barns, distant fields and ponds, and the gazebo near the solarium dining room. Winter-wood was indeed picturesque and peaceful.

A man crossed the street and entered in a side door to the town offices, a German shepherd by his side. Was he that the guy Veronica had nearly run over with her SUV? His boots left mud prints on the sidewalk. She had brought her own hiking sneakers, neatly aligned beside her slip-on Mary Janes, although she didn't intend to do much exploring. Perhaps hit the pavement and that was it. Okay, there. She'd do that. Tomorrow morning, a walk it was.

She settled on the bed and glanced at her phone. If she stood in just the right spot, near the corner window, she got a bar of reception and could read her email sporadically. At check-in, the receptionist informed them of the wireless availability in the media room, but she hesitated to hop online with spying eyes around.

She shifted her position until two bars emerged. She found herself on Julie's old Instagram page, but it wouldn't let her scroll down beyond the first several posts. One of Julie's last photos was of her standing in front of a glacial lake in Patagonia, wearing her bright yellow parka and the world's brightest smile, the kind that went to her eyes. The kind that would make a grumpy stranger's frown turn upside down. The kind that would bring light to Charlotte's days.

Rubbing the pain tightening her throat, Charlotte swiped out of the app and went to her email.

She waited while her inbox loaded. Nothing. Not that she expected anything new from Esteban.

This was going to be a long week.

Four

Time moved like a snail. The old-fashioned clock beside Charlotte's bed ticked loudly. Putting down another paper, she rose.

Her stomach growled. It was past lunchtime and granola bars were not cutting it. Gorgeous sunlight streamed in.

Go.

Yeah, yeah, she responded to the voice in her head. Sometimes she gave it Julie's voice. She knew she wasn't insane. It was her conscience poking.

She slid into her sporty Mary Janes, with socks. "Not cool, Charlotte." But her feet were always cold. Who cared? She put on her zipper fleece and a light vest. The forecast had said it would be sixty degrees. Indeed, a glorious April, but a constant chill resided in her bones.

At least the mayflies hadn't made their yearly appearance yet. Give those nuisances a couple of weeks. She wasn't sure how an avid outdoors person like herself—well, her *former* self—could not handle bugs. Mosquitoes devoured her. She was envious of friends who didn't blink an eye at them. She smoothed on sunscreen and organic bug repellant anyway.

The scent of baking bread wafted to her as she crept down the steps. Quiet conversations and light laughter emanated from the kitchen. Two kids ran past her in the front hall in a whoosh of energy. "Sarah! Jackson!" a woman hollered, rounding the corner, quick on their heels. "Omphf! Sorry," she said to Charlotte.

She smiled at the frazzled woman. "No bother."

The woman scurried after the kids, and Charlotte stepped outside.

Veronica was right. It smelled fresh and pure, like a new day. Pleasant as it was, her room held a trace of mothball mingled with the scent of old quilts and cedar furniture, so this was a literal breath of fresh air. Charlotte found a smile parting her lips as she turned toward the shops. The bar across the street was silent in the midday sun. She crossed Maple Run Avenue and strolled past the town offices.

Heart palpitations gripped her on the walk. When was the last time she just walked? Not a hike up a mountain with Julie, not a run along the trails near her home, not sightseeing in a foreign town or city. Just walking. She stumbled on a minuscule sidewalk crack and righted herself.

Her knees buckled, and she gripped the nearby streetlight's pole. Taking a few deep breaths, she refused to allow irrational anxiety to seep in. This was a walk, in a quaint New England town. "I'm on vacation," she chided. She drew upright and passed the feed store. The sign for the café was a beacon to her senses. She crossed Main

Street, needing something substantial to fill her hollow stomach and to warm her soul.

A maple aroma awakened her senses as she stepped inside.

No sign of Veronica or Josh. Those two had probably slipped back to their room for afternoon delight, forgetting her coffee.

"Hi, have a seat anywhere. Be right with you," the woman at the counter said.

Charlotte slid into a booth near the front window. She hated to sit alone, idle. Her fingers always needed to be doing something. More like she needed something to distract her from other thoughts. She could use a good book.

Having only two bars of reception, she skimmed the phone photos instead of scrolling socials. She had deleted most of the photos a few years ago during a night of deep sorrow and pathetic grief. Of course, she had backed them up on an external drive and in a cloud server. "Lame," she said to herself, tucking the phone into her pocket. Pamphlets sat next to the salt and pepper shakers shaped like cows.

She opened a pamphlet on the history of the town. Hmm. Apparently, the Millstone Inn had a rich history. The inn used to have a grist mill dating back to the nineteenth century. The mill used waterpower from the Mad River to turn stone rollers which turned grain into flour. She recalled seeing some of the historical tools in the front hallway of the inn. Maybe she'd check that out more, too.

A woman with a wide, welcoming smile greeted her. "Thirsty or hungry?"

"Both."

"Sweet or savory?"

Charlotte's stiff shoulders relaxed with the easy conversation. "Not sure. What do you have?"

She handed her a trifold menu. "Everyone's been asking for creemees with the nicer weather."

"Creemees?"

The woman laughed. "Soft-serve ice cream. With maple syrup on top, of course."

"Yum. Perhaps something filling first. Something hot? With coffee. Have any special flavors?"

She ordered a maple spice latte, hot, because she didn't like to jump on the iced-coffee summer bandwagon. She preferred a slow drink of dark java. In her mind, it was still winter. Per the woman's recommendation, she chose a turkey bacon grinder. Customers came and went, but her friends were absent. She sighed. She was going to have to keep herself busy this week while those two carried on with their activities.

She licked her lips, a nervous habit, and then robotically smoothed on lip balm.

She ate quietly, observing the comings and goings outside the shop. Perhaps she *would* take a walk later with her camera. Or...maybe tomorrow. Baby steps.

After perusing the souvenir shop, she poked into the bookstore. A chime on the door jingled overhead as she crossed the threshold. She made a beeline for the first stack of books on the table near the front. Books by local authors, Vermont memoirs, and bestsellers adorned the square table.

"Good day to you. Looking for anything special?" an older gentleman behind the counter greeted.

"Fiction recommendation?"

A twinkle glimmered in his gray eyes, and he scratched his gray and white salted beard. "What kind of fiction?"

Her cheeks flushed, and she coughed. *Scottish romance where the kilted Highlander gets the lass?* That last book she read had been a good escape. Instead, she said, "Surprise me." There were no happy endings in the real world. She had to stop reading those sorts of books.

He pointed to a stack beside the register. "Vermont author here. Kramer. She writes twisted mysteries."

A knot formed in her throat. She'd had enough with mysteries. "Maybe less twisted?" What *did* she like anymore? Not thrillers or murder mysteries.

"YA? Fantasy? Lots of that," he said with a nod toward the far wall. "Also, some local poets, in that section." He pointed to a small display.

Yuck, no. "I'll keep looking. Thanks."

As if walking under hypnosis or in rote routine, and with a book on Vermont wildflowers tucked under her arm, she found herself in front of the travel section after a few minutes. It was like she couldn't help herself.

She slid her finger along the alphabetized books. The beautiful scenery on the covers stirred old feelings of adventure. She drew her gaze lower. Australia...Europe...South America. She paused, a finger on the book for Chile and Argentina.

"Eh, you've found my favorite section," a kind, accented voice said from beside her.

She jumped and muffled a surprised squeak. In her doing so, coffee popped through the drinking hole on her to-go cup, splashing on her vest.

"Oh, sorry. Didn't mean for that to happen," he said.

She pulled a paper napkin from her pocket and dabbed at the vest. Thankfully, it was fast wicking. "I-I should know better than to bring a coffee into a book-store. At least my book is okay." She offered him her best smile. It was the dark-haired man Veronica had nearly killed.

"Good as gold," he said, his own face brimming with sunlight and smiles.

She nodded at his odd response. He had gorgeous dimples. Two of them. And he was handsome on closer encounter, too.

He added, "Your vest. Reputable brand. We sell that at the outfitter. That spot will disappear. You like to travel?"

How long had she been gawking at this section of books? "Sometimes."

"Here for vacation, I reckon?"

She belatedly placed his accent. Either Australia or New Zealand. Dark, serene eyes beheld hers, waiting.

"Yeah, with friends. Staying at the inn."

Why was she feeling so awkward? She went to feel her ring on her finger with her thumb...but the ring wasn't there. That old habit would not die even years later.

A dog barked, and the man crossed to the back door. "Reka, sweet girl, take your nap. Only a few hours here and then home, okay?" He spoke to her like a father to a toddler. The dog barked again. "A swim and walk this morning weren't enough for you?"

He approached the dog, petted it, and whispered af-fections.

Charlotte made a soundless "Aww" and kept perusing.

The man returned, nearer. Residual sweat traced his brow. He pointed to a selection of books in the middle.

"These are the best. Depends on what you're looking for though. Honest reviews or glorified fantasies?"

"Honest reviews, always." She chewed her lip.

He stroked a hand through his neck-length black hair, the longer top layer falling over his forehead. He knelt and selected a few books from the lower shelf. "You could go with the popular or famous names, sure, but I like these authors." He handed her one.

A book on South America sat in her hands. She muttered, "Thanks. Don't need that one."

"Oh, already been there, eh? All good, all good." He took it and shoved it back on the shelf. "Where do your dreams lie then?"

She swallowed and didn't correct him. *No, I wasn't there in* that *way. I was supposed to have been there for fun. Five years ago. I had gone for other reasons.* Instead of speaking that painful truth, she said, "Well, Vermont for now."

"You're in luck. I'm from Winterwood and know the best places to visit. The lesser-known paths tucked away in the mountains." His grin deepened the pair of dimples edging his mouth.

With that accent, and she surely decided it was New Zealand...she found herself stumbling over words. "You're from—" But she cut herself off.

She didn't doubt his authenticity at being a local, with the muddy boots that surely the elderly gentlemen at the counter might scold him about and equally muddied hiker's pants, a worn-out T-shirt, and open flannel. He even had a trace of mud on his neck. Not that she was admiring his smooth skin.

"I'm a Kiwi," he confirmed her retracted question. "What gave me away?"

"Ah...New Zealand."

He didn't seem put off, the smile firmly planted on his face. He pointed at the shelf. "You have plenty to pick from. I take it you're here for tramping?"

"Excuse me?"

He scratched the back of his neck. "Hiking?"

"No," she said too quickly. She sipped the last drops of her coffee. *Tramping*, that's right. She'd read that in a New Zealand guidebook somewhere. Usually her near-photographic memory was sharp. This guy's enthusiastic conversation threw her for a loop. Well, he *was* cute and friendly, and she was on edge. She blew out a breath to steady the chaos within. *It is just a conversation, Charlotte. Get a hold of yourself.*

"A traveler," he began, with a subtle but polite glance at her attire, "who goes to small town bookstores and likes books on flowers?" He pointed to the book under her arm. "Good one, by the way. Gorgeous photographs. A bit early for wildflowers but I can point you to a few meadow trails to see the flowers and birds."

"Why are you so interested in my comings and goings?"

Okay, now this just felt uncomfortable.

"It's my job."

"Huh?"

"I'm a tour guide, so I learn what my customers like. I also work here."

"Ah." That made sense. Her pulse settled.

He cleared his throat. "Well, I'm here if you have questions. We've got it all in our quiet area of the Mad River Valley. Covered bridges, goat cheese, cows, creemees, mountains." He meandered to the register and stood by the elderly man. "Sorry I'm a little late, Crandall."

The man nodded. "Always happy to see you, Matiu," he responded. "Boots out back, please."

"Been living in these things lately. Sorry, boss." He went out, changed his boots, and returned to the counter.

"I'll be back at three." The old man waved and left.

Charlotte's attention returned to perusing the shelves, her eyes unfocused, her mind a storm. She snatched the first book her hand fell upon.

She made her way to the counter.

His smile couldn't get any larger as he held the New Zealand guidebook she had chosen. "Choice! Way better than our neighbor across the ditch. Better footie team, too." He typed the prices into the register. "World traveler, beyond Vermont?"

Wow, he didn't let up. This man sure was chatty. "Used to be." The words slipped out before she could take them back.

"New Zealand has plenty to offer. Lupins in November. Good whitewater after the snowmelt. The Southern Alps." He bagged both her books, and she paid.

"Thanks."

"You're welcome. Cheers."

"Have a good day," she said, leaving.

His dimpled grin was infectious, and she found herself slightly mortified at her blubbering responses. Time to get back to the inn and hide.

Five

After dropping Reka with Nora, Matiu made his way to the inn for his dinner shift. The morning paddle had gone okay given the inexperienced clients. They only tipped the kayak once. At least there were no trampers to drag off the muddy mountains. He called that a win for the day. He was always willing to move SAR efforts to the top of his list, but lately the rescues were people not using common sense rather than the usual calls of runaway teenagers or wandering elderly.

His muscles were sore with the early spring white-water as the mountain snowmelt and runoff swelled the rivers. It was a good sore. Being outside was invigorating after a long winter.

The highlight of his day had been the bookstore run-in with that attractive woman. She had been guarded, but receptive to conversation, not the typical tourist visiting for leaf-peeping in autumn or to hit the slopes in winter. He liked the summer folk, the trampers and naturalists.

He wondered what her story was. Granted, not all the tourists were stereotypical elite Bostonians or New

Yorkers looking to spend a weekend in the country. Many came from all over New England: families, trampers, old-timers hungering for R&R. Those were the ones he enjoyed catering to. And he got a sense that woman could appreciate the simplicity of nature. He just got that vibe.

He popped inside the rear entrance of the inn and glanced at the dry-erase board in the kitchen.

Tonight's menu included pork tenderloin, goat cheese spinach salad, and a fruit tart.

Nate came into the kitchen. "Hey, Matiu. I was thinking we'd change the dessert to a lemon pavlova tonight. Impress the flatlanders. You've got a flair for pavlova."

Matiu put on his apron and washed his hands at the sink. "No worries."

Nate clapped a hand on his back. "Love your enthusiasm. I visited the gourmet grocery in Burlington today, got the key ingredients. I'm going to miss you next year. I've appreciated your added talent to our menu."

As quickly as Nate had come, he left. The others in the kitchen were busy chopping and washing. Nate was well aware of Matiu's plans to leave after this season. In this first year since reopening, Nate had done an amazing job updating and running the Millstone inn. It was the right thing to do to tell Nate about his plans of leaving as soon as he had been sure. But *was* he sure?

It was time. Home called. Kura wasn't getting any better. Home screamed for him some days. Everything reminded him of home. Bird calls at sunrise. Fog threading through the mountains. The slice of paddle in the river; the spray of water hitting his face. The crunch of twigs or pebbles beneath his hiking shoes.

Sure, he'd been in the United States for a decade, but he had moved here in his early twenties, wet behind the ears and eager for the American experience. These days, he was chock full of memories of his mum, dad, and cousin's family tramping about the mountains and lakes back home. Oh, how he missed it. Vermont's peaks were sweet as, and he had taken trips to the Whites in New Hampshire, but they didn't compare to home. He had never found his place here, try as he might. Maybe that was why he felt so restless.

He moved mindlessly through the pavlova, which would be done by dessert time.

Dinner passed in its usual fashion, the kitchen more stifling this week. Summer would be worse. As he finished washing dishes, a server, Becca, poked her head in. "Nate's asking for you."

He wiped his hands on the apron and exited the kitchen toward the dining room. A few guests had started a fire in the back pit, and the light flickered on the solarium windows.

"A couple guests wanted to commend you on the pavlova. Told them it was made by my resident Kiwi. Come," Nate encouraged, leading him in.

"Not a bother. I should head home," Matiu protested, although it was only nine p.m.

"Your modesty will get the best of you," Nate said.

Nate was not one for fanfare. If a guest asked, he would be happy to oblige. Matiu couldn't fault him for that. They were in the tourist industry, and pleasing guests was their job.

"Here he is—Matiu." Nate introduced him to the first table of guests.

Matiu nodded. "Good evening, ladies."

"Your dessert was delicious," one cooed. The other, eyeing him in a not-so-subtle way, said, "I'd love a personal tutorial."

Nate had already moved on to chat with a group at another table.

"We saw you walking in town, and then Nate told us how you're on the search and rescue team, too," she admired, licking her blood-red lips. She lifted her champagne with pointy purple salon nails.

This had nothing to do with the pavlova. He gathered his best grin of acquiescence. "Yes."

The other leaned on her forearms, her cleavage, well, cleavage-y. "Is that a hard job?"

"Must be. Look at those arms," the brunette said, reaching toward him. He sidestepped and straightened his posture.

"Matiu," one drawled, "where's a nice place around here for some fun?"

"Try Finnigan's next door." These women were in the wrong town if they were looking for the party crowd. They'd have better luck finding campers to enjoy s'mores with.

She moaned, pressing a finger to her lips and batting larger-than-life eyelashes. "I was thinking something more intimate."

"Thank you for the praises on the pavlova. Hope you enjoy your stay in Winterwood," he said with a stiff nod and a bite of his lip, muting less kind words. He returned to the kitchen to clean up.

He'd ditched the hookups and online dating apps years ago. There were plenty of men in town who would pounce on such opportunities in a heartbeat. Finnigan's wasn't a sleazy place at all, but if they wanted a one-night stand, that was the place. He used to enjoy it. But after too many dates with women in love with his accent or complexion, he had drawn a line. He was too old for this. He was pushing his mid-thirties already.

Half an hour later, he left through the rear entrance, and instead of heading toward home, he trudged onto the wraparound porch that ran along the side and toward the solarium, a beer in hand. A throng of guests had congregated around the firepit. He needed a quiet moment before shoving off. He fell into an old rocker on the Victorian porch and mused, sipping...and simmering.

He thought he was alone when an easygoing voice said, "You work here, too?"

He turned. The brunette from the bookstore huddled in a chair. She'd been lost in the shadows when he scanned the porch a moment ago.

"I work a lot of places," he said, not hiding the edge in his voice.

Silence. He sipped. Okay, he should have been nicer, but after the ruse at dessert, his temper had flared. He reeled it in.

"Where's your dog?"

That surprised him, and his mood softened. "She's home. My neighbor watches her when I can't bring her to work."

"Sweet dog."

"Her name, Reka, means 'sweet' in Māori. She lives up to her namesake."

He tossed back the beer, sullen, replaying the encounter from the dining room. Those types of women were always hungry for more than dessert. Finally, he said, not turning, "Why'd you buy that book?"

"What book?"

"The travel one. New Zealand." Okay, he was baiting her, itching for the fight. Another gulp.

"Oh...New Zealand. Used to be on my bucket list."

"Used to be?" She had said that, too, about traveling while in the bookstore. In the porch light, she quivered. "You cold? I can get you another blanket from inside. The firepit is going. You can head back there, too."

"No, it's okay. It's quieter here."

"I like the quiet, too." He sighed at his behavior. He had let those women get under his skin and needed to snap out of his foul mood. "I'm Matiu." He cleared his throat. "Matiu Christiansen."

The strain in her posture released. She took a sip from a mug, the coffee's rich, nutty scent floating to him on a draft. "I'm Charlotte MacGregor."

"Nice to meet you, Charlotte. A bit late for a coffee."

"I don't sleep much."

"Night owl, eh? I'm more of an early bird."

"Doesn't Reka miss you? You seem busy."

He freed a tightness in his chest with a deep exhalation. "Yeah, she does."

"Sorry, I didn't mean to imply—"

"It's okay. Parental guilt," he said with a light laugh.

"I feel the same way with my students sometimes."

"You're a teacher?" He rose and moved to a closer rocker, being sure to respect her space. He always gave people a few feet of comfort room. He'd learned that quickly in the tourist industry.

"Yeah." Her words were a ghost of a response, hardly a whisper.

The shadows played across her defined features under the ocher porch light. In the bookstore, she'd had a natural allure. Light complexion, warmed by days outside, wavy brown hair to her neck and shoulders. Only a trace of blush, no fancy nails or expensive shoes. In the dark, she appeared hunched and...sad.

He took a sip and encouraged relaxation into his overworked muscles and mind. The bitterness had seeped in. He had to stop doing that. People liked Kiwi Matiu, friendly, smiling, charming. If they only knew how sorely he yearned to leave this place. His mother had moved to California after his father's death. He couldn't handle the fast-paced urban life though, so he stayed here. Vermont was laid-back.

Belatedly, he said, "Sorry, didn't mean to pry. Not supposed to consort with the guests." Nate had warned him before—a few times in fact—but this was not that type of *consorting*.

"It's okay. I like talking about my students. I teach high school science."

"Science. That's choice. My father used to work at Vermont State University. Taught and researched meteorology and astronomical sciences."

"Wow, good school. I have a student who loves meteorology. I've suggested that college to him. What does your father work on, specifically?"

A coldness wrapped around Matiu, and his flannel didn't abate it. "He passed away. He studied cutting-edge meteorological technology for measurements in harsh environments."

"Sorry, didn't—"

He waved a hand. "No worries."

Her eyebrows raised. "Harsh environments?"

"New Zealand is home to those—volcanoes, hot springs, alpine mountains."

"Cool. Did he ever visit Mount Washington in New Hampshire?"

"Yup, he got to spend a winter there once."

"That's impressive," she said. "Wicked winds there."

"Do you really want to travel to New Zealand, or did you buy that book because..." He bit his lip and internally slapped himself. Man, he was an egg tonight! He wasn't sure why it was taking him so long to calm down after that dining room interaction. He shifted in his spot to leave but didn't. "I mean, just..."

"I get it. No, it wasn't your accent," she said with a light tease and chuckle. She swallowed a gulp of her coffee. The hesitation hung thick in the air, but she finally said, "I'm a hiker. Well, I used to be. My sister and I used to hike a lot."

All those "used to's" had him truly wondering what they were about.

"Ah, your sister? The woman at dinner with you?" He doubted that well-primped beauty did outdoors anything.

Charlotte laughed. "Oh, Veronica? Gosh, no. She's a skier; that's about it."

Stars had begun to emerge in the navy-black sky. He needed to get home to Reka. Maybe he'd pull out his dad's Dobsonian telescope and stargaze. The telescope was huge, as tall as him, and weighed like eighty pounds. He had to roll it out on a wheeled stand. Less light pollution here meant better skies.

His breath a cloud of mist before him, he said, "She may get her wish for snow. There's a storm front approaching. Might hit our mountains later this week, but the lifts are closed for the season. She can do some snowshoeing."

"The only shoes Ronnie likes are designer." She hugged herself and rose. "I better head in."

He stood, too, with heavy reluctance. "Me, too. Maybe I'll see you around tomorrow. Small town, everyone knows everyone."

She nodded. "You seem to be everywhere."

"You can say that again. The mountain calls me in the morning. Hopefully no bros getting stuck."

"Oh?"

"Mud season."

She tapped her foot. It was cold, and he kept her. He kind of enjoyed the chat and didn't want to leave though.

"Oh, mud season. I read about that. You work on the mountain, too?"

"Yup. I've got a long résumé." He scratched his head. "Bookstore, cook at the inn, trail mucking for the US Forest Service, search and rescue volunteer—Reka's my partner; I'm her handler. I'm a backcountry guide, too. If you're interested...pop by North Sports. Ask for Jacques, the owner."

She mumbled, "Sure."

Had he hit a nerve? That wasn't the most enthusiastic response for a hiker.

He lowered his voice and said kindly, "Pō mārie."

"What does that mean?"

"Peaceful night to you."

"Ah. *Pō mārie*, Matiu," she responded, her voice smooth as cream.

"Got the code to get in the back door?"

"Yes, thanks."

He inclined his head and shoved off, dropping his beer bottle in the recycling bin outside.

Six

After another restless night's sleep, Charlotte summoned herself from bed at six a.m., groggy. As birdsong echoed through the open window, she stretched. The room was crisp and invigorating.

She had to get out. Aside from dinner, Veronica and Josh had been no-shows all day yesterday. She presumed she'd need to self-entertain again today. First things first. A walk. She could get another coffee on her way back if the café was open. She quickly dressed. On a whim, she grabbed her digital camera.

The inn was tranquil at dawn as the staff prepared breakfast, and she slipped outside. A buttery yellow sun nosed above the horizon as she turned onto Maple Run Avenue. A few pickup trucks and a dairy delivery truck rattled down the road.

She decided against earbuds and tunes and opted for Mother Nature's sounds instead. She missed this. Just being. Not beating herself up or keeping herself busy so that feelings didn't come to the surface. Just walking, taking in her surroundings, appreciating the calmness of dawn.

She succumbed to a warm peace as the sunrise transitioned to a deeper orange. She pinched off her lens cap and snapped away, framing the town in the camera's viewfinder. Though bare, the trees would be lush with green foliage soon. She looked around. Rolling hills, meadows, farmland, and the mountains nestled the town in a bubble of splendor.

The quietude urged her on, so she continued down the road.

Her hikes with Julie had always been an escape from the concrete and metallic urban world. The beauty of Winterwood brought a flood of happy memories, the small-town hallmarks quite similar to her hometown in central Massachusetts. Even the long grass and weeds to her right reminded her of late nights catching fireflies in the fields.

After paper-grading and mindless internet surfing last night in the media room, she had flipped through the Vermont wildflower book until past midnight.

It now sat on the dresser, left open on a page with pansies.

It made her think of Julie. Instead of slamming it shut, she had let it sit open. She had traced her finger along the beautiful purple and yellow petals. Such a pretty, happy flower.

Charlotte was a weeping willow to Julie's pansy.

Sigh.

She had kept the New Zealand guide in the shopping bag, unwilling to read it. New Zealand had been next on her and Julie's bucket list...after Patagonia. The lure of the colorful pictures within the book was too much. She just...couldn't. It would send her down that path again.

Fatigue finally triumphed at one a.m. It seemed her lighter-dose OTC sleep aid was losing effectiveness. She still woke up at sunrise.

A spiderweb speckled with morning dewdrops caught her eye. She knelt, adjusted the camera settings, and snapped, the rhythmic, reliable click soothing to her soul. Hearing the jingle of a dog collar with a bell, she stood.

Of all the people, Matiu approached from down the block.

His voice carried on the still air. "Kura, cripes, why aren't you in bed yet? It's late there. Listen. You need to go to bed. I'll be home soon. *Soon*. Then I can take care of you and Jacob. You're my *whānau*."

Matiu didn't notice her. Charlotte capped her lens and fidgeted from foot to foot. He had been coming her way but then paused and stared off into the hills, his forehead wrinkled.

The dog broke from his hold, the leash dragging on the sidewalk, and she ran toward Charlotte. Matiu didn't even turn to see where the dog had run, too consumed in his conversation. He thrust an empty hand through his hair, clearly frazzled by something.

He paced and turned away in the opposite direction.

Charlotte supposed he knew his dog wouldn't run far.

"He needs a man around, too," Matiu said, almost grinding the words out.

He nodded in a brooding sort of way.

Charlotte felt like an intruder, but the dog, Reka, approached her.

Charlotte held her hand out. Reka sniffed it and sat patiently, her tail tapping the sidewalk. Charlotte stooped to her level. "Hello, Reka. Sweet thing, he calls you. How's your morning going?"

Reka barked once and pushed into Charlotte for more petting.

She obliged, rubbing the dog behind her ears and along her strong back. She was a beautiful dog with a thick dark brown coat and intelligence in her eyes. Charlotte grabbed the dangling leash, just in case Reka decided to bolt.

Matiu's voice drifted over. "It's late. You should be resting." He picked up a piece of trash on the sidewalk and pocketed it while listening to the person on the other end. "Yes, I'm sure. I need to be there for you." More listening. "Yeah." He practically sighed the word out. Another nod. "I'll suss it out." He paced. "Love you, too," his lead-thick voice came, like the words burned to say them.

Charlotte's ears warmed. "Go, go," she encouraged Reka. Perhaps she could turn around now. The corner wasn't too far away. Reka barked again and didn't leave her side. It was too late to hide behind a bush or something, and she would feel bad to drop the leash and let Reka run away.

Matiu shoved the phone in his back pocket and finally turned his eyes to her. It was as if he broke through a haze as he closed their distance. Gone was the wrinkled brow, the stressed voice, the hunched shoulders. "Hey, Charlotte." There it was: his smile. Two glorious dimples carved beside a wide happy-to-see-her smile.

Heat flushed her neck, and she was grateful for the high-zipped collar.

She shifted her look to Reka. "She wandered over. Didn't want her to run away..." She handed Matiu the leash.

He swallowed, his dark brown eyes soft. "A*ta mārie*, good morning. Ah, and uh, thank you. Reka's good. She won't run far." He gave Reka a treat from his pocket. "Sweet girl."

He scratched her behind her ear, and she looked at him with the love of a dog who adored her owner.

Matiu shifted his attention back to Charlotte. "What's on your itinerary today?"

She shielded herself, irrationally, with the camera dangling from her neck. She swiped errant hairs from her face, then played with the camera strap. Gosh, did he think his charisma worked on all the ladies? Well, it *did* work. She had seen those two women drooling over him at dinner and him smiling, enjoying. She wondered what this Kura must think. His ring finger was bare.

"Not sure," she finally said.

"Want to join my kayak tour this morning? We have room. Reka and I were heading over to the outfitter."

"No thanks."

"You can invite your two friends, Veronica and...," he said, running a hand through his thick hair. His smile broadened.

Did this man just wake up smiling?

"Josh," she said for him. She yearned to turn on her heel and retreat to the inn. "No, no thanks."

"How about one of the mountain trails? Some other time?"

"I don't do mountains."

His brows rose, and he scratched his cheek. "What tramper doesn't do mountains? I thought you liked mountaineering and travel—"

Her pulse soared. "The kind who doesn't do mountains," she said, her voice cracking. She hated talking about this. *Change the topic, Charlotte.*

He gave her a dubious nod. "Okay. There are plenty of flat trails around..."

This man was persistent; she'd give him that.

She pressed her lips together. "It's not th—" She stopped herself. There was no point in explaining. "Just, no thanks."

"Ah, okay. Offer stands if you change your mind. "Are you heading this direction?" He pointed back toward the inn.

"No, the other way." She stepped away a fraction, gesturing toward the café.

"Okay, see you around."

He was off, his gait quick to keep up with a dog eager to move. Feeling like a fool, she watched him walk away.

Routinely, Matiu worked his morning shift at North Sports. The kayak tour had been canceled, so he was stuck inside, stocking shelves and running the register. He was still a bit rattled by his phone call with Kura this morning. She would not listen to reason.

Stubborn as a stone, as his mom would say.

He was no different though.

Kura had been his best friend through childhood, their families close. While drugs, gangs, and alcohol had been prevalent in their community, she had found her way and had a fulfilling, albeit demanding career as a nurse and was an amazing mum.

He, on the other hand, had been restless, teetering on the dark edge with a few rough friends. Bad blood ran deep between some Māori. Kura had encouraged him to move to the United States at twenty-two with his parents, to seek education and exploration elsewhere. Not that he couldn't have done it in New Zealand; in fact, he had gotten accepted into choice universities, but his home had always been with his family, and when his parents relocated to Vermont, it only seemed logical to come, too. So, Vermont it was for college and for life. It had been hard to leave Kura behind.

He had settled in well enough, tried to make a home for himself here. The mountains had sucked him in, too.

Then Kura got married and the bastard, Matiu's former best bro, had cut and run, leaving her when she was at her worst to be a single parent. Now, her MS raged, and he needed to help her. It was the right thing to do. He hated being so far away. She was also his *whānau*, his family, his home. Dad was gone. Mum was across the country. Nothing kept him in Vermont anymore.

Mum was on board with the plan to move back to New Zealand, so all would fall into place.

"Careful, Matiu!" came Jacques's voice. "Not Mount Everest big."

"Sorry, boss." Matiu adjusted the stack of gear that was close to toppling. He'd taken the camp stoves, flash boilers, coolers, and fuel canisters and made a mountain of sorts. He had over-stacked during his ruminating.

Sometimes he wondered what life would have been like if he had stayed in New Zealand. Would he have gone to uni there?

A bit scattered today, his thoughts shifted. He secretly hoped Charlotte would stop by. She was not the usual tourist. She seemed to be put off this morning by something, too, but he wanted to see her again, nonetheless.

At noon, he grabbed Reka from her bed behind the counter and headed to the bookstore for his afternoon shift. He leashed her in the back and refilled her water dish.

Yawning, he entered through the rear door.

There stood Charlotte at the register, more books in hand.

A renewed vitality filled him as if he just chugged a shot of espresso, and he made a beeline for her.

"*Kia ora.*"

"Excuse me?"

"Hello," he said. "Again."

Her look went back to the card reader as she entered her pin. "Oh, hi. *Kia ora.*"

For a tramper, she did a lot of bookstore visiting. There was so much more to see in Winterwood and the Mad River Valley. Why read when you could be *in* nature? The sunshine was great today, and the temps soared. He was bummed he had been stuck in North Sports instead of paddling on the river.

He sized up the books on the counter in front of her. He tapped the top book. "Choice. That author used to live in town. An early explorer of the Green Mountains."

"Hmm." She remained angled away from him, her brown hair falling into her face as she dug into her back pocket for something. She pulled out a lip balm and applied it.

He leaned on the counter and gave Crandall a nod. "Left the boots with the pup, boss."

Crandall's face stretched with a soulful smile as he handed Charlotte her reciept. "Thanks, Matiu."

Matiu continued, rambling and curious. "For a woman who doesn't tramp—uh, I mean hike—or travel, you sure like to read about it," he mused, but then wanted to kick himself. There he went, being a dope.

She nodded to Crandall. "Thanks." She brushed past Matiu, cool and almost angry-like.

He followed her. "Was just teasing. My mum says I'm really good at putting a foot in my mouth. Sorry. Do you kayak? Or is water also not your thing?" The foot got lodged farther up in his throat. If it could just kick his brain! He had to stop this pestering.

She laughed, lightly, but a pink bloom rushed to her cheeks as she continued to the door. "I like water, but I probably shouldn't. I also don't do rapids, and isn't that what the Mad River is famous for in spring?"

The knot in his chest loosened at her breezier response. At least he had chipped away at some of that ice. Was it him? Or was she just having a bad day? "Yup, more with all the snowmelt and runoff. Lots of class two and three. We can put in downstream from the sizeable ledges, steer clear of the rapids though."

She didn't respond.

He walked beside her. "Hey, where's that camera of yours?" He didn't stop to let her answer, afraid that she'd shoot him down again. "I have tomorrow morning off. Would you like to join me and Reka on a paddle on the river? I can take you to see places in that book," he said, flicking a thumb to her bag. "Great lighting for photos. Placid water. Might work your muscles, but no whitewater."

She paused at the shop door. "Look. It's your job to be nice to us tourists. But…" She rubbed her nose and turned her gaze away but not before he saw her hazel-brown eyes blink back tears. She said with a fractured voice, "I didn't come here for…" She stopped, hugged her arms, the bag of books tight against her chest. "I just came to be alone. Sorry, no. Anyway, your wife probably wouldn't approve." She turned to leave.

He grabbed her shoulder. "Whoa! What? I don't have a wife."

She sniffed. "That's not what it sounded like this morning."

He dropped his hand from her shoulder as if he'd been zapped.

"Huh?" He scrubbed his chin. "Oh. That's just Kura."

"Okay, your girlfriend. Whatever."

"No, no. That's my cuz, Kura. Honest to G."

"Who was Jacob?"

Ah. He processed it quickly as he recalled what he'd said on the phone this morning. No wonder she was skittish. He hadn't been exactly quiet on that phone call either. "My cousin's son. He's like a nephew to me."

"I don't think—" she stammered.

He took her elbow. Why did he keep touching her? "Just a paddle. Reka's a great guide. It'll be heaps of fun." One more no and he would stop. She obviously had no interest in him or kayaking. He released her elbow slowly.

She didn't step away. "You have a kayak for her?"

"Of course. Parental requirements," he teased.

There it was. A smile parting her lips. She sighed and loosened her death grip on the paper bag of books.

He shifted tactics. "I'll take you to the non-tourist places. Off the beaten track. Free of charge. No rapids, I promise. Reka doesn't like them either. Bring your camera. Really. Some great spots, good light."

She exhaled, sweetened coffee breath floating to him. "Why?"

"Why what?"

"Why are you being nice to me?"

He shrugged. "It's just a paddle on the river. And I could use company. You seem to like the outdoors. Reka doesn't talk much. That's all."

And I sorta like you.

Light returned to her face as she took a moment to respond. "Okay. Gentle water?"

He nodded. "Promise. I'll pick you up at the inn, say eight a.m. tomorrow?"

Fine lines crinkled the sides of her eyes. "Okay," she breathed. She strode from the shop, the bell on the door chiming as she exited.

Seven

Papers graded, curriculum finished, and her presentation on first aid training updated, all Charlotte had left to keep busy were the books she had purchased. The local autobiography was okay, but when the author got to a story about a famous accident on the mountain, she slammed the book shut.

She texted Veronica.

After a trip to the café for coffee and pastries, her friends disappeared for some alone time—again.

Soon, late evening was upon her, and Charlotte found herself outside. The porch was more embellished than last night. The window planters were filled with early spring flowers, and a large pot of pansies sat beside the front door. Of course...pansies. She almost shook her head at seeing them, but then she paused, and felt the tiniest smile stretch her lips.

Matiu turned the corner and approached her from the rear of the inn.

"Evening," he said. "Or rather, g'night." He was toting a tray with two teacups on saucers.

"Good evening," she said, strangely euphoric to see him. He *did* have a melodious voice, and she enjoyed his company, even if he was almost too chatty, too eager. His smile was contagious. The distraction did a great job competing with her inner demon.

"No firepit again?" he asked.

"Nah." Though the heat would be appreciated, the smoky air from one always triggered memories of camping with Julie. So, the porch it was.

"Didn't see you at dinner but saw you here," he said. "Thought I'd take a chance with some tea."

"I was in my room." *Eating leftover pastries and reading.*

"Missed a goodie tonight. Want me to grab you a plate? Roasted duck and pearl onions with creamed spinach."

"No, thanks."

"You're going to need fuel for tomorrow's paddle. First, a cuppa," he said, handing her a tea.

Herbal fragrance tickled her nose as she accepted the tea served in the delicate teacup. In the cooler air, steam rose.

"Thoughtful, thanks."

"Nate has decent teas, but I keep my secret stash at home."

"Where's home?" she found herself asking, taking a sip with a soft guttural sound. "Hmm, this is nice, flavorful, but...I'm more of a coffee drinker," she said with candor.

"That means you have not found the right tea yet. Wasn't sure if you were a lemon or milk person. I went with milk." He grinned, sipping from his own cup.

He had to stop doing that. His smile charmed the heck out of her. She sipped. "Good choice."

An attraction to him would be perilous. She had to keep cool, keep it friendly. This was not why she had come to Vermont. But who was she kidding? She already liked him.

"I live a few blocks away. I have an apartment above an older neighbor, Nora Wakefield. She watches Reka for me when I work."

"That's nice of her."

"Well...there's a story behind her affection for Reka."

"Oh?"

"Mrs. Wakefield was one of my rescues."

The shock must have shown on her face, for Matiu was quick to add, "Nothing scary. She wandered away once from the senior center on a walk. Most of our rescues are really searches, usually the elderly who went out and got turned around, or lost track of time. And their caregiver or family member reports them missing."

"Ah."

"Sometimes it's dementia, Alzheimer's. Not Mrs. Wakefield though. She just got too adventurous and ended up disoriented on a trail near the senior center. She lives in a house in town, and I rent an apartment above. She loves Reka."

"I don't blame her." She sipped the tea. "So, the people you help are mostly old ladies who have gotten lost?"

"Sometimes. I've seen my share of runaway kids or those dealing with addiction or mental health issues. People think SAR teams only respond to risky mountain rescues, but it's rare to deal with those with today's technology. Better cell phone coverage, GPS, apps on phones, or in some cases, we can guide a person down via phone."

She nodded as he continued.

"However, if someone is injured or dehydrated, then that's when we go up the mountain to do a full-blown rescue. With mud season, some cowboys get it in their minds that they don't need to listen to Mother Nature. Sometimes we gotta scoop them out. Nothing dire. Twisted ankles, or people caught in bad weather. Poor planning. Cocky egos. People think they're invincible, but the mountain has them beat."

She knew he meant it in good humor, but it packed a punch. She swallowed and switched subjects. "You've been in Vermont for long time?"

He puffed a breath, filling his chest, then releasing. "Moved here about ten years ago. I'm going home soon for a visit."

Her jangling insides quieted. She shifted, all too aware of the feeling his closeness arose within her. "Oh, to visit Kura?" she said, giving away that she had heard his entire conversation.

"Yup. How long are you in town for?"

"Through next Wednesday." What day was it already? They had arrived Wednesday evening, so it was Friday. Time was dragging. She didn't want to return to the bookstore tomorrow for yet another book. Maybe the library? Ha, that wasn't any better. Where else could she go to kill some time?

She wasn't sure what else to say. It had been a while since she had dated or had a nice conversation with a guy. *This guy is just a guy*, she reprimanded her inner psyche. A nice Vermonter from New Zealand with adorable dimples, to-die-for accent, handsome eyes, with a knack for conversation...who was *just* being friendly and showing her around. That was all. Tomorrow's kayaking on the river was just that. Nothing more.

He was silent, drinking his tea.

Sometimes she liked the silence. Sometimes it ate away at her spirit. If she was busy, she couldn't stew with remorse. Silence forced her to confront those inner demons head on.

She was about to speak when he rose. "Well...I have a pup to give cuddles to. See you tomorrow. *Po mārie*."

" 'Night."

Yes, just a nice guy. That was all.

Eight a.m. came and went. Then eight thirty. Charlotte rose from her spot near the inn's carport and drop-off area and fiddled with the cuff of her sleeve. She swiped through her phone, mindlessly looking at social media, though the Wi-Fi wasn't much better outside.

She should have given Matiu her phone number.

The same elderly couple who had passed by her half an hour ago must have returned from their daily walk. She saw them yesterday, too. It was sweet to see them holding hands.

The woman gave her a look of...pity?

Charlotte smiled back, then clenched her teeth and shoved shaking fingers into her pockets. Her stomach hardened. Matiu wasn't coming. She pulled out and rolled her lip balm around in her hands.

Had it been a charade? He had seemed genuine and honestly into her. Was she imagining things?

Perhaps he *was* married, and he lied. Tourists could be fools. She could be a fool. Tears stung her eyes. This was stupid! She was over lying, cheating men.

She went inside. Veronica called from the dining room in the back. "Charlie!"

Charlotte desired nothing more than to rush to her room and toss herself beneath the covers, but she walked into the solarium. Josh was nowhere around.

"Oh, honey! Did he not show? Bastard," Veronica said, pursing her lips.

"Shh," Charlotte said with a glance over her shoulder as she plopped into a seat.

Veronica waved a hand at the other guests eating breakfast. "Nobody cares."

Why had Charlotte texted Veronica about this? Oh, yeah, that's right, because she was her best friend and Charlotte had been excited. The attention, his handsome smile, and his *something*...had been a front to either get in her pants or acquire business for his tour work. Though he wasn't remotely close to garnering either yet. Irrational Charlotte spoke these lies, but Understanding Charlotte knew he hadn't been out for a quick lay or anything nefarious.

Regardless, he had stood her up. She sniffed. "So much for that." Charlotte eyed Veronica's coffee mug. She blinked away blurred vision.

"Perhaps something came up."

Charlotte nearly snorted at the innuendo, her thoughts a whirling storm. Usually, Veronica was the one with her mind in the gutter.

Veronica chuckled at herself. "Oh, not like that. I saw those vultures eyeing him the other night. He had zero interest in them. In fact, I saw him checking you out," she said smoothly. She dropped two sugar cubes into her coffee and bit into a croissant.

"You're imagining things."

Veronica poured her a cup of coffee from the carafe on the table. "Drink. Something came up."

"You can stop saying that."

Her friend's bright blue eyes widened. "Oh...Charlie, girl, what a mind you have. Look, you told me about him. He's a busy guy. Works a million jobs. There's a logical answer. Just text him."

"I don't have his number." Charlotte chewed her lip, sipped the coffee, and poked at a melon on Veronica's plate. She mindlessly traced a floral design on the fine linen tablecloth.

"Don't go there," Veronica ordered through a mouthful of food. She pointed her fork at Charlotte's face.

"I'm not."

"Yes, you are. Not all men are like Sean. He was a controlling ass who couldn't keep it in his pants. There are better fish out there! I thought I'd never find somebody, you know. Damn," she continued, lowering her voice, "I'm nearly thirty-five and *just* married. I've seen my share of jerks and players. But there are good fish."

"Everyone leaves."

She dropped her fork with a clink on the plate. "And...you're *there*. Stop. Stop now, okay?"

Why settle for good when you can have great? Sean had said. Curse them for having been high school sweethearts. Curse him for not being faithful. Curse him for controlling everything in her life, including trips with her sister—or *would-have-been* trips.

Be it death or affairs, everyone she loved left. Sean. Julie. Other men who saw her damaged baggage and ran for the hills. Even Veronica. Well, she wasn't *gone-gone*, but Charlotte sure felt like a third wheel on this vacation.

Mom and Dad and her brother seemed to have moved past the loss of Julie or at least had found better coping mechanisms. They weren't gone like Sean and Julie, but they felt *distant* these days.

Veronica snapped her from her sulking. "Stop it. I see it on your face. Besides, we're only here for a few days. It's okay to let loose and have fun. No attachments. He'll come." She chuckled again. She sighed with a wave of her hand. "Have fun. Accept his apology. Because I guarantee, with the way he was looking at you, there will be a big apology coming."

"No attachments?" she repeated, feeling childlike.

"None."

After breakfast, Charlotte retreated to her room and did what she always did when moping. First, she checked email on her phone from the one corner of the room where she had two reception bars. Ugh, this Wi-Fi was cruddy!

Nothing from Esteban nor from the other resources she had tried in Chile. She had contacts in four towns. Why would today be any different than any day before it? She was delusional to hold on to hope that information about Julie would just magically appear in her inbox.

Next, she clicked on her photo folder on her phone, which was better than Julie's Instagram page. Then, she scrolled through the folders from each hike she and Jules had taken, starting with the high school ones. She and Julie had been drawn to hiking—everywhere.

Back then Charlotte had been madly in love with Sean, giving him all her heart. Then in college, she had fallen from the clouds when the real Sean emerged. Sean didn't like the outdoors. He'd rather work himself to the bone...many late nights and business trips away.

Only they weren't all *business*.

She wallowed and cried with the pictures and memories, a deep longing for not just the thrill of bagging peaks or exploring backcountry, but for the sister she had lost. "I'm sorry, Jules."

Julie was gone, missing, disappeared...and suspected dead. If it hadn't been for Charlotte's narcissistic liar of a husband, she would have been with her sister on that trip five years ago in Patagonia, Chile.

Julie was dead, and it was all her fault.

Eight

Matiu hightailed it to the inn.

Ah, hell, he screwed up. Charlotte was probably angry. He was an idiot. Damn his schedule...and scattered mind.

Jared, who worked at the registration desk, wouldn't divulge a guest's specific room due to privacy and all that, but Matiu thanked his luck. Charlotte's friend, the strawberry-blonde woman—Veronica—was on her way out with her bloke on her arm. Jared was nowhere in sight, so there'd be no inquisition.

"Hey, I'm looking for—" He stopped in front of them.

"Buddy, she's upset," she said, poking her finger into his chest. "You better have a reason for standing her up."

He nodded to her. "I do."

"And?" She crossed her arms and tapped her toe.

"I was working."

She narrowed her blue eyes.

"Really." He needed to make things right with the soft-spoken, mysterious brown-haired bookstore woman. He wasn't taking Charlotte on a paddle for tip money to fatten his savings account. He genuinely wanted to take her around. He liked her.

"Don't break her heart, or I will break your bones."

The man with her—a quick glance showed a ring, so he must be her husband—coughed. "Ronnie…"

She turned to him, her voice honeyed. "What?"

"You're not her mother."

"*Hrmphm.* I'm her bestie." She cocked her head to the side and raised her eyebrow. "Got it? No fooling around. If you're not serious about seeing her—"

"I am."

"Then treat her well. And apologize big."

"Yes, ma'am. Got it."

"Okay, then. I'm no ma'am. I'm your age. You make me seem old," she said thickly, tartly. "She's in room eight."

He took the steps two at a time, feeling gutted. He'd fouled things up…if there had been anything to foul. He paced the hallway, not a sound emanating from Charlotte's room. After a long moment, he brought his knuckles to the door. As soon as she opened it, he blurted, "I'm sorry. I didn't forget. You're pissed off."

Her face was ragged, the glow he'd seen in it yesterday…gone.

"Wise assessment." She half hid behind the door. She had the throw quilt wrapped around her upper half even though the inn wasn't cool or drafty today. "Couldn't have left a note or something?"

He ran a hand through his hair. "Can I come in?"

"Don't think so." Her eyes were strained, tired, and the green luster in the hazel was dulled.

"I didn't forget or ditch you. I have too much stuff going on. Got pulled into mucking this morning at like six. I didn't know if you'd be awake or ready, so I thought it unwise to just show up. A mate here, banging on your door at the crack of dawn? I switched my shifts. Crandall doesn't require me at the bookstore this afternoon. How about we give that paddle a go?"

"I'd rather not. Thanks."

She began to close the door. He stopped her by stepping into the doorway but not walking in. "I was going to text Nate but the reception sucks on the trails. Honest to G."

"Who?"

"The owner. Text him to let you know." He sighed. "However, I'm not supposed to consort with guests. Eh, anyway, before long, it was noon." He was blabbering.

"Maybe you should follow Nate's advice. You're a busy guy. You don't need to show a *flatlander* like me around in your free time."

Ouch. "I want to."

She hugged her arms closely but didn't retreat. He noticed her plate on the side table. Did the woman never eat in the restaurant? He'd bet his last dollar that Liz, Nate's cousin, was the one to bring a plate of food to Charlotte. They didn't offer room service but Liz had a heart of gold and went the extra mile.

He kept with it. "Wind has died down. The paddle will be sweet as. Reka's waiting in the car. She likes you." *Guilt her with the dog. Good one, Matiu. I like you. Please forgive me.*

Her shoulders drooped, and she spun away from him. "I'm not looking for...for...this," she muttered.

"Not sure what you mean."

She turned fully away. As she looked down, her long lashes swept over her eyes, creating a curtain of shadow.

He shivered from her palpable pain.

She emerged from the quilt and tossed it on the bed with a huff, snapping out of her melancholy. "Maybe you have a girlfriend or wife and don't want to tell me. Fine. I'm not like that. I don't do *that*. Those women the other night—I saw how they flirted with you. I'm not in town for a one-night stand, okay?"

Ouch more. It pierced his heart. Is that how he came off? As a skirt-chaser? A player?

He scrubbed a hand over his face. He softened his voice instead of letting her incorrect observations rile him. "I'm not out for a one-off, *err*, one-night stand. Friends? That's all. A paddle, Charlotte. Or Charlie. Is that what Veronica calls you?"

She turned on him and clenched her jaw. "Charlotte is fine."

"Kura is my cousin. That's all. No girlfriend or wife." Why did it hurt to verbalize those words? Not that he hadn't tried to settle down with a woman. It was...well, nobody ever embraced him, the full, true him, messes and ambitions and all. His girlfriends had always tried to change him to suit their needs. They had sought to take the Māori out of the mate. He dislodged that thought with a shake. He kicked the braided rug on the wooden floor.

He was about to leave when Charlotte shuffled her socked feet, straightened her back, and changed her demeanor in a heartbeat. "I could use air. It's nice today. Next time, find a way to let me know, okay?"

His heart hung on the words *next time*. There...she was almost there. Happiness rushed through his skull like a storm front. He wiped sweaty palms on his pants. She wanted to come. "Need a waterproof bag for your camera?"

There. The edge in her face softened, her cheeks rounding into an almost smile. Sunlight broke through the squall in his chest. He'd take it. His spirit lifted.

"That would be nice. Let me grab my shoes."

Realizing that he was now all the way into her room, a guest's room, he backed away. "I'll wait in the hallway. I've got lunch, too. Made some sandwiches," he said, belatedly. "It's a short drive to the calmer parts of the river. I have two kayaks. Some scroggin, too, delicious stuff, homemade."

"You lost me."

"You might call it granola or trail mix?"

"Ah, yes."

"Sorry, can't take the Kiwi out of me after all these years." Tourists loved it...but he didn't mention that fact. Perhaps that was why the women never stayed. Once they learned the true Matiu, they got tired. No more charismatic New Zealander. Just him. Plain old him. He blinked, swallowing the admission like burnt toast.

She paused, frank sincerity shining in her eyes. "Nothing wrong with that. You should be you."

"Can I carry anything?" he offered as she came to her door a moment later, camera and backpack in her hands.

She shook her head. "I've got it."

"Got any gumboots?"

"Any what?"

"Boots. For mud."

"Nope." She nudged a toe forward. She wore hiking sneakers. "Do I need them?"

"The mud would swallow those shoes. I have a spare pair in the car. Might fit you."

They made their way downstairs. Nate flurried past, talking with Liz. He paused and gave Matiu a cursory glance of warning. Matiu said, "G'day, boss. See you this evening."

Nate's brow was curled with curiosity. Matiu mouthed *all good*, held the door open for Charlotte, and they were off.

Reka barked from the front seat of his Jeep.

"Back," he said with a scratch behind her shoulder. Reka hopped into the back seat, and he tossed her muddy towel beside her. He gave the leather seat a swipe with his hand. "Sorry, my US Forest Service vehicle is in the shop. When I do trail work, I take their vehicle, but today I had to drive mine."

Charlotte slid in as Matiu held the door open. "Hi, Reka."

The dog nosed her head between the seats.

He drove down Main Street, then left, across the covered bridge, then north. A few more turns and he was on a side road to take them to his favorite boat launch area on the river. The wind whistled through the kayaks and the rack holding them in place. The straps danced, but the kayaks were tightly secured. The breeze and sunshine felt heavenly today.

The dirt road to the put-in was bouncy and muddy, and Charlotte jostled beside him as his mud-worthy tires sloshed. He rounded a larger rut, but she fell toward him briefly.

"Sorry, bumpy road."

He smiled, and she did in return. She pushed herself upright, her hand briefly using his knee as support. He did not mind.

"It's like sticky oatmeal," she said.

"Great comparison. The best trails are off the trodden road."

"I agree."

He turned slower.

"What's with this mud season? Never experienced this in Maine or New Hampshire when I've visited."

"The mountains are softer, with less granite. The heavy winter snow thaws, mixes with spring rain, and boom, mud. It's sticky nasty stuff. They call it the fifth season."

She laughed. "I can see why."

"We don't recommend tramping—hiking—on the Long Trail, or any of the trails from early April until Memorial Day—our mud season, but many people, usually tourists, don't heed the warning. I get the pleasure of helping, then reprimanding them about their poor decisions."

"That explains the shovel and two by sixes in your back seat."

"Yup. Knock some sense into them," he said in jest.

She muffled a laugh. "You're a busy guy. How many jobs *do* you have? You mentioned quite a few."

He scratched his head. "Well...my search and rescue work is volunteer based, but they only recruit highly trained people. Our authority is the VSP, the Vermont State Police. Calls come into emergency operators at the Middlesex Barracks, get filtered through a unified command structure, and are steered toward the proper destination and agency. Commander Joaquin Bixler, he's VSP, handles that responsibility, and my friend Greg is the assistant team leader, and he's part of the US Forest Service, too."

"And all as a volunteer?"

He rubbed his chin. "The use of civilian resources varies from state to state. Some states refuse to use civilians, though they have competent volunteers. Here, our teams are a mix of state police and civilians."

"Do you have a lot of certifications?"

He snorted. "That's something that peeves us a bit. No state certs are required in Vermont. They use the resources who get the job done, and that's it."

"Wow."

"We do have some K9 certs. For myself, I get the usual certifications in first aid, canine handling, land navigation training, crime scene preservation..." He trailed off.

She shifted in her seat. "Very interesting. I have first aid training and teach courses on CPR and crisis intervention for our school district. Not real exciting."

"No need to make light of what you do. Every bit helps, to keep people safe."

"Yeah. Your work sounds adventurous," she said, her voice holding a despondent tone.

"Sometimes. It's not perfect, but the incident command system is an improvement from a few years ago. It's a unified team effort of both jurisdiction and function. Usually, I help disoriented folks. Like I said, elderly, runaways, and such. Not too many rescues. Mostly searches."

He scratched his head. "Can't remember what else I told you. I muck and do trail maintenance for the US Forest Service. The bookstore a few hours a week, like you've seen. The inn on Thursdays through Saturdays, and sometimes other days to help Nate with prep or work, but usually in the kitchen as cook. Plus, I work for Jacques at the North Sports Outfitters, stocking or giving tours..." He left off that laundry list of jobs. "Wow, I do too many things."

"You *are* busy."

So much so that I had to blow off picking up a gorgeous, friendly woman like you for a paddle on the river. He scuffed a hand along his chin. He'd forgotten to shave this morning.

He shifted topics. "You'd like the science behind it," he said.

"Behind what?" She lifted a brow. He cut the engine as he parked in a spot not far from the put-in.

"The mud. It takes a special kind of soil to make muddy roads. Twelve percent fine soil content, they say."

He slid on his boots, pocketing the jandals for when he got near the water. He handed her the spare gumboots from beside Reka.

"Thanks."

"You can change into your kicks once we get to the edge. We'll take the boots along in the boats."

She slid on the boots and nodded, her hair falling in waves around her face.

"Anyway, Vermont has the perfect percentage of fine soil for muddy roads, and two-thirds of our roads are dirt. Likewise, the trails. Hence, the perfect soil, the result of glaciers and soil percolation, lots of snowmelt and rain, and you have the magic combo. Toss late-season snow on top of that, and you have a recipe for disaster if anyone decides to traverse the ridge in it."

"Very interesting. Did you study science in college, too? Like your father?"

"Yup. I majored in environmental science and business."

"Both seem handy for your profession." She paused. "I have to ask…"

"Go for it."

"Why so many jobs? I mean, with your degrees and abilities you could pick one and settle somewhere. Do fieldwork through a research organization or…"

"Teach?"

Her cheeks flushed pink. "I'm sorry, I didn't mean—"

"No worries. I guess I have my father's restless spirit. Although I've been in one place for ten years, I get fidgety doing one thing. Maybe I have too many passions. Plus, well, I must make ends meet. Multiple jobs patchworked together is maybe not the best long-term goal."

"Sorry, I didn't mean to imply anything. It's great."

He offered her a smile. "It is great. No offense taken. All good." He hesitated to tell her more. Soon he would be settling down with his own business in Queenstown. Maybe he'd find the right woman to tame his spirit, too.

You can't settle a restless spirit. It was his mother's voice.

His father had been eccentric, lost in troves of books and research. After he had exhausted his resources at Victoria University in Wellington, they had relocated here, to the heart of meteorology country. His father had even gone to Oklahoma for a year for an extreme weather research project, then returned to Winterwood shortly thereafter.

Matiu was like his father. Perhaps his young rebellious days were still with him...but instead of riding the road of troublemakers, he chose to be restive in his ambitions. He heaved a sigh with his over-analyzing.

Now was not the time to ponder his choices in life. He tossed a smile to Charlotte. "Ready to have some fun?"

Nine

"Do you mind tightening Reka's harness and grabbing the paddles and life jackets from the back seat while I get the boats?"

A familiar gloppy muck greeted them. Matiu meandered around the Jeep, leaving sloppy prints with each vacuum-like sucking step. He usually wore socks, like Charlotte was, but his toes needed to breathe after days in the boots.

She set to work assembling the paddles. After untying the straps, he lowered each kayak into the nearby longer grass and away from the mud. His personal boat was heavier and longer to accommodate Reka.

Charlotte was already strapped in her life jacket by the time he had both boats down. He'd given her the pink spare he kept for clients. She looked cute.

"Here." She handed him his. He put it on and dropped the paddles into the kayaks.

Without needing to give her instructions, she grabbed the end of the kayak by the knotted rope handle, and he did the same, and they brought one, then the other, to the put-in. She paused as he situated her kayak first in the water. "She'll be right," he assured.

"Huh?"

"You looked nervous. It'll be all good. Hop in. I'll hold it steady. Oh, wait. Slip off the boots. Chuck them in the bow and put your hiking shoes on. My boots slip off the footrests if I wear them. Too clunky. Narrower-toed shoes work better."

She paused, a beleaguered frown twisting her mouth. "What's up?"

"It's—" She heaved a sigh. "I know what I'm doing...but it's been a couple of years. I guess I'm nervous."

She didn't do mountains, which he found odd for a tramper. Now she had second thoughts on the water, too? Reka paced nearby, muddying her paws and brushing against his lightweight pants.

"The river's quiet today, and this is an easy paddle. Would you prefer we do something else?" he said to pacify her.

She leaned on him as she took off the boots and swapped for the shoes, all the while keeping a hand on his shoulder to steady herself. She stepped in after tossing the boots in. "No. This is good."

He gave her kayak a thrust, and she began paddling. Reka hopped aboard his boat with his whistle. Through the years, she and he had formed a bond, a groove. They were nearly a symbiotic unit when on rescue missions. Sometimes he wondered if she was the only female who would tolerate him. Reka understood him. Then again, he also brought her salmon and bacon after work. He wondered if that trick would work on Charlotte...

A grin cracked his face, and heat rose in his throat. Bloody hell, it had been *too* long. He wasn't going to live his days with only a dog as companion in his bed.

He took off his boots, plopped them inside the kayak, and submerged into the river in his jandals, the coolness of the water biting his ankles. "We'll paddle downstream. It's easier if you keep to the side. Reka's a trained search and rescue dog, in case." He grinned.

"Thanks," she said sarcastically.

He sensed her nerves smoothing as paddle sliced water. Sunlight speckled the chop, but it was overall a serene ride. The paddles sloshed with each cut. Birds called, and the occasional sound of a passing car filtered through the trees from the main road. As they distanced themselves from the launch and drew deeper into the forest, he lost himself to the serenity.

The trees had hardly sprouted for the season, but in a matter of weeks, the area would be thick with leafy silver maples, black willows, boxelder, and American elms. The riverside vegetation was brown and green, that ugly period between winter and spring. Today had been another unusually mild day. He'd take it.

He cracked his neck. The mud was unbearable on the mountainside at times, and the spring-break tourists were demanding. People needed to escape the claws of winter, but Mother Nature often retaliated.

He resumed his tour guide persona. "They call it the Green Mountain National Forest, but we're not so green yet. Still brown. Crunchy, muddy." *Snap out of it. She's not your typical tourist.* She was probably already well-versed on all this stuff. "Have you been this way before?"

"First visit to Vermont. I've gone to the Whites a lot. Franconia Notch, the Presidentials, and seen my share of Maine, mostly coastal with my family, but I hiked inland a bit. I do love New England. You?"

Hmm. So she did go hiking? Or used to. Not anymore? Why? He said, "Been to New Hampshire a bunch. I also did a stretch of the AT from Maryland to New Hampshire with a few mates. Never got to start in Georgia. Too much commitment. Can't do the four or five months it takes."

"And you seem to be a busy guy."

Her words unknowingly stung. He swallowed the pain. "New England is home to a lotta prime peaks. So I am content here. Been anywhere farther?" He hadn't got a clear answer to that from her.

She chewed on a pink lip as she paddled, her focus on the horizon. "Hopped around the country, saw some national parks in my teen years with my family. Did the road trip thing. Hit the notable ones."

"That's choice. I'd love to travel farther. I've mostly stuck to the East Coast. My mum lives in California now near San Diego. I've only visited her twice since she moved. Never had a chance to explore the Sierras or mountains out West. Plenty of surf if you dig that sort of thing."

She rested her paddle across her lap for a moment, allowing the current to help her along. "I'm sure New Zealand is beyond comparison to any of this."

He smirked. "Well, not to sound snide, but yes, it's heaven on earth. We call it Godzone for a reason. Have you been abroad, out of the country, I mean? You mentioned New Zealand on your wish list. Been anywhere else?"

She shifted in her seat, no longer reclined against the back support of her deeper hulled kayak. Finally, she said, turning her eyes away, "Nowhere fun yet."

"Bucket list, right?" he added.

"Yeah."

"Guess teaching limits your schedule."

"It does."

He didn't prod further, but added, "If you do head abroad, Aotearoa is the place for mystery and beauty."

"The land of the long white cloud," she said with awe.

"You've been reading that book."

"Nah, I've read about it before. I'm torn between Australia and there."

"You know where my vote lies. No need to go across the ditch. Too many snakes and creatures that can bite you in Oz."

She laughed. Her eyes were full, round, soulful.

"If you ever go there, drop me a line." Why did he say that?

"Oh, when you visit? Do you travel home to see family? Spend longer stretches there?"

He cleared his throat. "Not as much as I'd like, but I'm visiting soon." *More like moving there, mate.* "I reckon you mostly travel in summer, because of school. That's winter in New Zealand, but you can still do a lot that time of year. November is sweet as. My favorite month. You like flowers, right?" He remembered her book purchase. He sure was rambling.

"I do."

"Gorgeous lupins in the Southern Alps. Near Lake Tekapo and Wanaka. Huge meadows of flowers set against the snowcapped mountains and glacial lakes."

"That sounds amazing."

Silence fell on their conversation as their paddles sliced water.

Charlotte was an agile paddler. She maneuvered shallows and held steady in the deeper parts, while circumnavigating the rocky shore or avoiding dead-wood in the river. He wasn't sure why she was humble or hesitant. She kept pace. A beaming smile joined the sunlight on her golden cheeks. She wore a purple hat, the kind sold at sports and outdoors shops, light-weight, brimmed, and fast-wicking, casting shadows beneath her dark-lashed eyes.

Now that he had a moment to watch her—because that's what guides were supposed to do, he told him-self—her natural beauty aroused a sensation within him he hadn't felt in a while. No red lips or slick, body-clinging outfits to draw attention. Nah, she wore lightweight pants, waterproof hiker shoes, a light T-shirt, and a vest over a nicely shaped chest. She looked like a model for an outfitter's catalog.

His chuckle drew her attention.

"What's up? Sorry, I'm slower. It's been a while."

"Having fun?"

"When does my tour continue? You've enlightened me on mud season and Aotearoa. What next?"

There, wow, a bigger smile brightened her face.

"Soon. See that nose of land up there," he said with a point to a marshy area along the riverbank.

"Yeah."

"We're going to pivot there and make shore."

"Make shore?"

He drew off his own cap, scratched his head. "Some of our tour is afoot. To let you rest your arms. That okay?"

"Sure."

They paddled nearer to the shoreline.

He said, "Did you know this river flows north?"

"No. That's interesting."

Reka jumped off and swam the short distance. She ran on shore and shook out her fur with a bark.

Though she had the right water shoe for it, for her shoes were waterproof and breathable, the type sold in North Sports, Charlotte nimbly sidestepped and avoided dropping her feet into the water. She made it ashore, dry, like a dancing pixie hopping among plants and cracking dead branches. She was darn attractive in it. He hauled the kayak in.

"Where to now, my guide?"

She didn't have a typical Massachusetts accent. Nothing wrong with that; heck, his own dialect was like a foghorn sometimes. "This way, there's an old stone cabin."

"Ah…" Her face lit. "Do we need the boots?"

"Probably." They switched shoes. He tossed his jandals and her shoes in the kayaks. She grabbed her camera from the waterproof bag.

They slogged through the early spring growth of long grasses and streamside vegetation. "I call this mud soup."

She giggled.

"Dead leaves and brown water. I can't wait for summer," he added.

"The brown gets to me, too. And there is so much snow. Meh!"

"Soon the best season will be here," he concurred. Today a light blue sky embraced them like a hug. "This weather is fine though. Been really warm this week."

"I doubt winter is done."

"Me, too. Forecast is calling for snow in a few days. More in the mountains than in town. We'll likely get a dusting in Winterwood." He inhaled the tangy forest scent. "Up ahead is a moose hunter's cabin. The original builder was likely a logger, too. The author writes about it in that book you bought."

A little farther through the forest and they were upon the old stone cabin.

Charlotte exclaimed, "Wow, impressive."

"As you can see the roof is missing, but it had a high ceiling, and massive windows." He gestured. Reka bounded ahead, sniffing. "Not far, Reka."

They stepped through the entrance, the doors and any shutters long since rotted away. All that remained was a shell of a cabin, but it had been robust, chiseled stone, and it stood solid and eerie in the forest. He entered, and Charlotte followed through the tangles of roots and shoots.

A decades-old oak tree grew from the ground in what was likely the living area or kitchen. Beside the tree stood, nearly intact, a central fireplace and chimney two stories high. Matiu stepped on acorn shells and lost his balance, unlike him, and fell into Charlotte. "Bugger! Sorry!"

She held his weight.

He paused, his hand on her arm, her exposed skin warm beneath his fingers. Reluctantly, slowly, he removed his hand. "Pretty sunlight today if you want to take pictures."

"Huh?"

He pointed to the camera slung around her neck, the lens still capped.

"Oh. Duh." She took off the lens cover and moved away from him.

She ducked, squatted, and shot photos from all sorts of angles, each step careful and deliberate. After a few minutes, she returned to him, standing there and, well, gawking. He clamped his mouth shut. What was with him?

She was luminous, her hair thick and wildly wavy from the slight humidity in the air, her face flushed with happy exertion from the paddle and walk, and eyes glowing with that love of nature he often felt, too. A naturalist like him knew that look. It was a high. Nature pushed the adrenaline through his veins and brought him to a peak of both joy and peace.

A part of him would love to share that pleasure with a partner...somebody to curl beside him at night in his bed, somebody to warm his soul and heart. Somebody who didn't have four paws and wet nose. Somebody who could appreciate the winter's radiant night sky, the early spring morning birdcall, the fog that curled around the mountains in the fall. Nature felt like the closest thing he'd have to a partner, besides Reka. The *maunga*, the mountain, was his home.

So why did he feel so lonely still?

She adjusted her camera so that it fell on her lower back and the strap crossed her breasts. "Ready to return? Or is there more to the tour?"

He was glad to have helped her turn the corner with whatever seemed to be bothering her. His no-show this morning hadn't helped. He was always overbooking himself these days. Too many plates spinning. He needed to leave Vermont. Not that starting his own business from scratch was going to be a break from the grind. It would keep him busy with something he enjoyed, something that was his. He'd be his own boss.

Maybe then he'd find the right woman who would settle down with him.

Too bad Charlotte didn't live in New Zealand.

He gulped that thought away. "How about tea?"

Ten

Charlotte dropped off her muddy shoes at the inn while Matiu waited in his Jeep. She hurried through her changing. Her pants were soaked since they had kayaked against the current back to the boat launch. Her arms burned. It felt good. Triggered memories. For once, in a positive way.

What to wear for tea with a guy? At his place.

"It's just tea," she reproached, slipping off her wet bottoms. Matiu was equally wet and didn't seem bothered. She presumed he'd change into something else for the dinner shift. She secretly wondered if the tea invitation was like the typical American coffee. *Hey, baby, want to come up for coffee?*

"Don't be ridiculous," she told herself while she swapped her sneakers for the clean Mary Janes. She laid the hiking sneakers on paper towels she'd asked for at the front desk. She'd let the mud dry, then flake it off and brush them clean.

It was the afternoon, and Matiu had only another hour until his shift at the inn.

A quickie then?

Good grief. That was Veronica's voice invading.

Thinking of those two lovebirds... They had to emerge from their bed oasis at some point, right? She'd already determined their daily routine: sleep in, late breakfast, sightseeing who-knows-where, then afternoon sex before dinner. Heck, she'd heard them.

Probably bored with the shopping in Winterwood, a town of only a few thousand, and during peak season she presumed mostly tourists, they had likely ventured north for more shops or tours near Waterbury or Montpelier. She was a bit steamed by the thought. What if she wanted to explore the shops, too? Ice cream, cheese, and coffee all ranked high on her favorites list.

She let the irritation slide away like rain droplets on a jacket. She had declined her friend's invitations afterall. It wasn't Ronnie's fault Charlotte was in a funk.

She snatched a look of herself in the mirror. "Horrid." She unknotted her hat hair with her brush. In a last-minute decision, she brushed on blush and lip gloss. What had gotten into her? This morning, she had been heartbroken about being left and now she was primping. She blew a breath and scurried to the lobby.

Matiu's dimpled grin met her at the Jeep. "You clean up nicely. Not that you were as muddy as me," he said with a point to his mud-splattered pants. He even had a trace of mud along his straight jawline.

She fought the urge to wipe it away...the neat freak in her, but also the one who desired to touch him.

Her heart hammered as he drove the short distance to his place. *You are not sixteen, Charlotte MacGregor. You are too old to play games! Have some tea, and just relax for once!*

Even thirtysomethings need fun. That was certainly Veronica's voice.

They'd already dropped the kayaks off at a storage area near the outfitter. "Mrs. Wakefield doesn't like a cluttered yard," Matiu had said.

She didn't blame his landlord. Charlotte's own apartment was immaculate, even if she only had a tiny rooftop garden and potted plants with zero grass to mow. Oh, how she missed living in a rural area. It hadn't been her choice to move to the city. That had been Sean, of course.

She had uprooted herself in her twenties after college and left her family. Granted, her family was only an hour away, and she'd met Veronica and Josh in Boston. She also loved her students, especially the quirky ones. While her parents were retired and living peacefully in central Massachusetts and her brother enjoyed the married-with-kids life, here she was, divorced and single, childless, at nearly thirty-five years old.

Oh, Jules, what has become of me? She'd become a ghost of a person since Julie's death and after the messy split with Sean. A soul without a home.

But.

This morning had summoned the fire in her. Was she ready to feel that part of herself again? Matiu's tender attention during their kayaking on the river had relit the flame. A flame that had gone from a weak pilot light to a strong simmer with each stroke of the paddle. It warmed her spirit to feel this way again.

She reached into her pocket and spread on lip balm, letting the sharp mint awaken her further.

Matiu turned into a street parking spot. A sharp whistle brought Reka from the Jeep. The dog's swim had kept her clean, and she had avoided the muddy spots at the launch on their return. Reka led the way up the steps to Matiu's apartment that was situated on the second floor of a two-decker. He unlocked the door. Reka rushed in and assumed a place on a worn dog bed.

Matiu cleared his throat. "Sorry, it's...a mess."

That was an understatement. His place held the homey feel, sure, but Matiu was a slob. It looked like a tornado had whirled through. Instead of triggering her neat-freak anxiety, Charlotte found it to be a strange but comfortable welcome. She'd always been tidy, and Sean had been strict with his regimen. If things weren't "just right," he flew off the handle. He had never hit her, but there were times she'd thought he might.

Five years later, she still found herself over-organizing and cleaning. She had to let that go. It was actually a relief to see Matiu's beautiful mess.

"Smells clean," she said with a grin.

"I make sure to not let the funk build. Open windows, air it out, ya know," he added as he weaved past the piles of outdoor gear—skis, snowshoes, heavy-duty backpack, and a dog vest with a bell—near the door, behind the couch.

She followed him to the kitchen. "That's a lot of gear. How often do you have to rescue people for real? I mean, on the mountain, not grannies or rebellious teens?"

Why could she not stop asking him questions about his search and rescue work? Well, she knew why. Julie was why. Charlotte needed to know all the details. Every last thing. Because with Julie...she knew so little. And it drove her crazy.

"More than I should. Our SAR team is getting tired of the mud trampers this season. We're winding down. Winter is our most demanding season. We coordinate with the ski patrol, unless we're needed in the backcountry. A surprise storm or unprepared trampers can lead to poor decisions and missteps. We've never lost anyone though."

"Ah." God, those words stung. Had Julie made a poor decision to keep hiking in a snowstorm in Torres del Paine in Patagonia? Was she one of *those* statistics? If her sister had gone off the path, and that was Charlotte's assumption, for she knew little about her sister's disappearance on the mountainous hike, then yes, it had cost her dearly. Sometimes, Charlotte's mind ran rampant, and she wondered if her sister had been abducted or worse or she had decided to fall off the radar of life. Jules would never abandon her like that though. Why would Julie want to deliberately disappear?

"Are you hungry for some Vermont signatures?"

She fished herself from her thoughts. "Sure."

He filled a tea kettle with water, then placed it on a burner. He rummaged through a hand-woven basket brimming with tea canisters.

"We have cheese. Lots of cheese. Protein, ya know?"

"I love cheese. That is gorgeous." She traced the red, yellow, and green pattern along the woven basket.

He followed the pattern, too, his fingertips briefly touching hers. "Nice, eh?"

She nodded, pulling her fingers back and moving them to her chin.

"It's *harakeke*. New Zealand flax. My mum loves to weave. Whenever she gets her hand on *harakeke*, she gets busy. She's always sending me stuff like I'm a young kid."

"Is it just you?"

"Oh, you mean brothers or sisters? I'm an only child. It's just me and my cousin Kura. She is my closest thing to a sibling. Though she and I are cousins, I consider Jacob my nephew."

He pointed to a stack of wrapped confections. "Mrs. Wakefield makes great brookies."

"Brookies?"

"A cookie baked in a brownie. Goes perfect with tea. It's a Vermont thing."

"*Ohhh*, let's have those. Cheese can wait."

"Choice. We can have cheese later."

Later. She fidgeted, and her stomach fluttered. Choice? That had to mean sweet or cool by his context. She filed it away into her memory bank.

"Grab a seat, and I'll be right there," he said with a nod to his couch. He cracked his knuckles as he collected mugs and plates. "I guessed last time, but do you prefer milk, lemon, or honey?"

"Milk would be nice, thanks, and a bit of honey if you have that."

He set the mugs and brookies on a platter. "Almost out of milk." He pulled a marker from a drawer and wrote on a dry-erase board on the fridge. "I know I'm messy but lists at least keep me organized."

"I love lists, too."

She snaked around piles of things on the floor, pushed aside a basket of what she presumed was clean laundry in her path, and fell onto the plush couch. An intricate quilt, which appeared Māori based on its design, was spread across the couch back. Drawn to the beauty and bold colors and swirling shapes, she traced the pattern. Gosh, why was she always touching things? She withdrew her hand.

He approached. "I'm a slob, eh?"

"Maybe."

"With my schedule, sometimes I feel hardly here."

She shifted his paper stacks aside to make room on the coffee table.

"Chur," he said, setting the tray down.

She thought that was thanks, like cheers. Deciphering his slang had proven to be like solving a puzzle. Interestingly, the more she was with him, the more his unique colloquialisms unveiled themselves. Perhaps he remained guarded with the tourists.

He gestured at the quilt. "My mum made that, too," he said, sitting beside her, leaving a half foot of space between them.

Make room for the Holy Ghost, a nun's terse reprimand from her Catholic school years came into her mind. She almost laughed at the random memory. "She's talented. What do all the symbols mean?"

He pointed to one shaped like a hook. "This is the *matau*, a fishhook. Symbolizes safe travel over water. Legend states that Maui pulled the North Island, Aotearoa, out of the water with a fishhook, that the island was a fish. The South Island was his canoe. We just call the whole place Aotearoa."

"I've read that. Which are you from?"

"North Island, Wellington area. We loved to travel south, near Queenstown. Don't get me started on north versus south with who is more Māori...bit o' contention there." He cleared his throat. "Eh, we know you're a reader, aren't you?"

"Indeed. Assessing," she said, mimicking him with a tap to her temple.

"Keen."

"I don't really assess, but I do have a nearly photographic memory," she said.

"That's a sweet ability." His dimples popped out again. "Quick. Close your eyes. Name all the gear I had over by the front door. No peeking!"

She eyed him dubiously, but found herself smiling and closing her eyes. She rattled off everything she had seen, down to the color or design of each bag or shoe.

"Wow!" His grin matched hers. They laughed.

He rolled a finger to another design on the quilt, a circular spiral. She followed with her own hand.

"Ferns signify regeneration, new growth. This is a *koru*. You see this symbol everywhere in New Zealand. Tourists love it."

He dug a hand into the neck of his T-shirt and withdrew a jade necklace. "This is the *pikorua*, a twist."

The urge to touch it made her fingers prickle.

"It's breathtaking." She shoved her hand beneath her knee instead and crossed her legs.

"My mum again."

"What does it symbolize?"

"Well..." He took a moment, clearly perplexed. He chewed on his bottom lip. "It's a strong bond between two loved ones. The arms twist, having no end...as relationships should. Unified for life. One endless connection."

Her breath caught.

He clarified, "From my mum, no wife or girlfriend, believe me, Charlotte. She gave it to me when she left for California. It was hers. My father gave it to her before they married. Though he wasn't Māori, he appreciated the culture and loved my mum fiercely. It can imply a maternal-child relationship, but she gave me strict instruction on its future." His dark brows lifted as he ran a hand through overgrown black hair.

She loved how he said her name. "Oh?"

"She told me I must give it to the woman I want to spend forever with." He tucked it in, his dark irises holding hers for a long moment.

"You'll find her soon."

"I do hope."

The kettle whistled, startling her senselessly. He grinned and rose.

She exhaled. Awkward moment broken.

"I have several teas."

"Surprise me," she said, swallowing the lump in her throat. She rubbed the infinity tattoo on her wrist, reminded of its own meaning. She and Julie had gotten the identical tattoo years before all their travel adventures. Best friends forever. At the time it was young and silly. Now, it was all she really had left of Julie aside from memories and photographs. Julie had never kept trinkets or material things.

The tattoo was a brand of eternal grief instead of being the intended symbol.

Matiu ambled back over to the couch.

While he brought the prepared tea kettle to the tray, she glanced around his messy place again.

"My place is an up-chuck of Māori and my country, sorry."

"No need to apologize. It's your heritage."

"My mum is full Māori, but my father was *pakeha*—European white—hence the surname Christiansen."

She nodded. "He came for work at Vermont State University?"

"Yup. My mum's also a professor. She teaches history and anthropology. She was happy here, too. They were a pair o' docs." He'd left the "f" sound off the "of."

He held her gaze.

"Oh, ha," she said slowly as she caught the joke. "Pair-a-docs...paradox. Got it." She almost snorted at his humor.

"After he passed away, she moved to San Diego to be closer to other family, and there are choice universities there."

"You're alone, then?" She didn't mean for it to sound pitying.

"I've got the *maunga*."

"*Maunga*?"

He pointed to the window, which highlighted one of the nearby peaks. "The mountain."

"You do."

"What's on your agenda tomorrow?" He gave her a brookie. He sat closer this time, his thigh brushing hers.

She unwrapped the brookie, grateful to have something to focus on, inhaled the enticing mixed scent of chocolate and buttery deliciousness, bit into it, and had to cover a moan.

"Choice, right?"

"I'm filing these sayings away in my brain. This is choice?"

"Yup or sweet as."

"Sweet as what?"

His dimples popped out with a smile that split his face. Did this man wake up smiling?

"Just sweet as. We leave the conjunction hanging there."

They shared a chuckle.

"Confuses the heck out of tourists," he added.

"Sure does."

"Easy as." His eyebrows lifted as he munched. "So, to-morrow?"

"Not sure. If Ronnie hasn't already gone there, maybe north to Waterbury to visit the cheese and ice cream shops."

"Nah, that's tourist stuff. How about farther off the beaten track?"

"You have better ideas?"

"Of course."

"What's your schedule like since you're Mr. Busy?"

His smile tipped to a frown. "Another full day. Since I mucked this morning on my day off, maybe they'll give me a break tomorrow. Plus, I'm waiting on their vehicle to get repaired."

She found herself nibbling on her lip, and it wasn't just from the chewy deliciousness in her mouth.

He poured her tea. His clock near the TV chimed. "I gotta change for the inn shift. Be right back. Drink the tea slowly. Let it work its flavor on your palate. Drink it like you would an expensive wine. Swirl it, inhale, savor." He rose. "Just don't spit it out after."

She almost snorted the swallow of tea. He was a charmer, even if he didn't know it. Maybe he did.

She admired his physique as he strode to his bedroom. The T-shirt stretched nicely across his wide shoulders, and she presumed he had a well-defined torso beneath it. She bet his calves were in kick-ass shape from all the work he did. And his butt...

He paused at his door. He tapped a gigantic black cylinder on a wheeled stand. It stood nearly as tall as Matiu and almost as wide. "Hey, Ms. Science Teacher, do you know what this is?"

She scratched her head, then noticed the finder scope sticking out. "Is that a telescope?" Her jaw nearly dropped.

"Yup. My dad's. A Dobsonian with a 12-inch aperture. Weighs like eighty pounds. On clear nights, I push it out onto the porch to stargaze. Maybe we'll have some clear skies and can look heavenward later this week? Do you like to do night photography?"

"It's been a while, but yeah. Sometimes." She nodded, awestruck.

He only half closed the bedroom door. She got a decent peek as he took off his dirty T-shirt. Elaborate, curved black tattoos covered his shoulder blade in similar symbols to the ones on the quilt.

She pulled her gaze away as he disappeared behind the door.

Veronica had warned her. *Fun only, fun only.* Oh my God, what the heck was she doing?

Eleven

The idea of dinner alone, again, in her room was disenchanting. Thankfully, Charlotte managed a last-minute reservation for the dining room. Veronica and Josh returned from their day's adventures and talked her ears off during the meal. Charlotte was happy they were having fun, and her frustration at being left behind—by her own choice—disappeared.

Whenever a person came or went from the kitchen, she straightened her posture and strained to catch a glimpse of Matiu.

Veronica caught her line of sight. "Ah, I see why you wanted to eat in the dining room. I take it your day was fun."

Charlotte's ears warmed. "We had a nice kayak on the river."

"Oh, did you?"

Charlotte swatted her friend's arm. "That's all."

After dinner, she retreated to her room, her mood buoyant. She had smartly exchanged cell numbers with Matiu before his shift at the inn. Instead of giving in to the voice in her head, telling her to look at more photos or videos from the good old days with Julie, she perused her lesson plans again. No wallowing, she scolded herself. It wasn't until she had come here, with limited wireless connections, that she realized how much she continued to search online, digging for any morsel of hope, while also gloom scrolling.

No more of that darkness. At least for this week. The anniversary of Julie's death loomed, two days away. She put her phone on the nightstand and took out her camera to review the photos she had taken today.

Matiu's text pinged at quarter past nine.

> Tea on the porch?

> Sure!

Cooler temperatures welcomed Charlotte when she went outside, wrapped in a small quilt from her bedroom. Even with her long-sleeved fleece, vest, and light jacket, she was cold. Her thicker coat—just in case—was in Veronica's car. She always overpacked.

She sat on the top porch step instead of in a rocker. Her breath puffed in a misty cloud before her as she waited. Again, the scent of a fire from the back pit infused the air. She traced the knots in the planks of the porch with the toe of her shoe, ignoring her thudding pulse.

Matiu shuffled through the side door. She rose to help him with the cups.

"Hi."

"*Kia ora*," he said, his smile deep and his teeth bright beneath the lamps. "It's colder tonight."

"You need a jacket," she said with a nod to his thinner long-sleeved top that clung nicely to his muscles.

"Nice quilt. I'll sit closer to you."

"I'm always cold. I won't have much heat to share."

"Logging in my assessment file." He tapped his temple.

She shivered from nerves as he settled beside her on the top step.

"Ya know, we could have tea inside," he suggested.

"I like the clear sky and fresh air. Night is my time, even if it's cold."

He nodded. "Clear skies are amazing. Perfect for that stargazing. I'm actually more of a morning person. I'm knackered today, so I won't be lugging big old Dob out tonight." He rubbed a hand on his thigh. "Oh, so I'm not sure about tomorrow. Neil's sick with the flu, and so is Kelly. They work on the search and rescue team, and Kelly also does mucking with us for the US Forest Service. I may need to cover her shift. Seems like the germs haven't left for the season."

"Nor the cold temps. Both tend to bite us in the ass in April." As if her body were agreeing with her, she shivered.

"I was serious. You going to share that quilt with me?" He inched closer.

"Nope. Get your own," she said, a bit giddy.

He pressed a hand to his heart. "Shot down!" Tea splashed as his laugh vibrated.

Her pulse quickened with the idea of sharing warmth with him.

He said, "That paddle got me sore. Bit more wind today than I'd expected. How are you feeling?"

"Equally sore."

He was so close. She subtly inhaled his natural scent. She couldn't place it. Probably his shampoo...combined with sweat and cooking oils. They sat quietly, unsure what to say next. His nearness upset her equilibrium, so she sipped her tea.

The door behind them opened, giggles emerging within a waft of strong perfume. Two women in short, curve-hugging dresses approached. "Oh, Matiu! There you are," one said, nearly drooling on her overdone lips. She slowed her step beside him so that her leg was mere inches from his face.

Charlotte coughed, their scent aggravating her senses.

"Good evening," he said.

"Come on over for some fun with *us*," the other said.

They lingered, reeking of booze already. The shorter woman tripped slightly—purposely?—and nudged her knee into Matiu.

"Enjoy your evening," Matiu said, not giving them a second glance. Instead, his stare was fixed upon...Charlotte.

Pitter patter, pitter patter. *Dang, heart, quiet yourself!*

"Come on, Matiu. Our friend Raquel told us about you. You're not living up to your rep, *mate*."

Turmoil mixed with the desire that had been building in Charlotte's stomach.

Matiu moved closer to Charlotte and placed a hand on her knee with a gentle squeeze, which she thought was him saying, *Hey, I'm not that guy*. His hand fed the spark within; her pulse pounded in her skull. Who the heck was Raquel? Was he really a player as she'd suspected earlier? And why did this make her feel so unsettled?

Not every guy was like Sean. Not every guy was an asshole.

"Cheers, ladies. I'm not interested. I'm all set."

The women relented and carried on across the street, mumbling to each other. "That's not what Raquel told us…"

Charlotte ignored them.

Matiu's hand still rested on her knee. "Sorry about that."

"Perhaps I should go. It's cold." She made to stand, but he didn't release his touch.

"Don't go. I can keep you warm," he said softly.

Quiet engulfed them.

A few minutes later, he broke the silence. "I took a while to settle in here."

Her pulse began to calm down.

He continued, "I don't…do *that* anymore. Maybe I used to while I was looking for myself. Now, I work, I sleep. I explore. Straight-up. That's all."

"Have you found yourself?" she asked, laying her hand upon his.

"I do each day when I'm on the *maunga*. There, the earth knows who I am. *Maunga* and I join in this spiritual connection. Hard to explain. It's frustrating being away from all my family, ya know?"

She nodded.

She heard him swallow as he flipped his hand over and threaded it with hers, palm to palm. He added, "I'd like you to know who I am."

She had no response.

He unclasped their hands and stood, taking the cups. "I'll text you, fill you in on my plans tomorrow."

She smiled. "I'd like that."

"Po *mārie*." His voice was smooth, sincere...like the warmest hug.

"Po *mārie*." She blinked and turned, unsteady legs taking her inside.

Insomnia joined her in bed, this time for a much better reason than usual.

Charlotte couldn't get his touch out of her mind. She wondered what it would feel like to be with him...those muscles wrapped around her, his lips upon her skin, their bodies in a bubble beneath his quilt.

Twelve

Matiu awoke early and went through his usual ritual. He texted Greg, who was the first point of contact for any SAR calls filtered down from Commander Bixler. The other two members of their four-person SAR crew, Neil and Kelly, were sick with the flu, confirmed by text messages. With the cooler temperatures, the mud had frozen overnight and would be a sopping mess this afternoon with warming.

He hoped nothing would happen in their sick crew-mates' absence. He had Reka, but all rescues were at least a two-person job. Plus, the helicopter crew, if needed. The helo was always a call away, outsourced from the Army National Guard or Border Control, but locating more ground crew would take time. Greg would relay all this to Commander Bixler, in case.

Experience had always taught him to be on high alert. His mind catapulting to the what-ifs and alternate plans, he flipped on the local weather on TV. Keeping an eye on weather was invaluable to all outdoorsmen. A part of him watched because of his father, too. Meteorologists were eccentric.

Though he was vastly different from his father in many regards, he could appreciate this.

The passion.

The forecasters predicted a cold front, with a possible chance of snow on the mountains and western ridge, a dusting in the valleys. Trampers needed to stay off the mountains the rest of the week. Mud plus snow could spell disaster. He needed to remain vigilant.

His window revealed Lincoln Peak and Mount Ellen standing watch over the quiet town, the bare ridge, the carved ski runs awaiting summer's wilds, the chairlifts empty. A lower cloud fogged in the summits, sweeping and misty.

Soon the Greens would bloom into their name, a tramper's dream. The sunshine and warmth this week had been a gift in an otherwise dull season.

Finished with his daily weather watch, he hopped online and perused his bank account balance. He was close. He could move by summer, push the date sooner. All his supervisors had given him the green light to leave when he was ready.

Not that he was an easy mate to replace with his technical skills and a SAR air-scent dog, but summer help would arrive soon for some of his jobs. The Vermont State Police canine unit had other dogs in training and had put the call out for more K9 certifications for the region.

Reka would move to New Zealand with him. Jack, one of the volunteer firefighters, was training his two dogs for SAR work. They'd be fine.

So why did he feel a bit off today while thinking about it? Nerves. That's all it was. This was a big change. A change for the better.

He stopped at Mrs. Wakefield's. It was early, but she usually didn't mind. After two knocks, alarm bells rang in his mind. No response.

Did she fall? Have a stroke?

She was in fair shape but was pushing eighty. Belatedly, her door opened.

"Ah, hey, Mr. Baldwin. Didn't expect to see you. Is she okay?"

"Matiu, how many times have I asked you to call me Ellis?"

Matiu acquiesced, though it felt weird, and said, "Sure thing, Ellis."

"Nora isn't well. I think she has the flu. I came over last night to take care of her." Reka pawed at the ground. "Need me to watch her today?"

"I can't ask that. She'll be okay for a few hours. I've got a date this morning."

A date? Was that what this was?

"Then definitely no bother. We'll take her. Get out and have fun. You're always working." His smile lines crinkled with understanding.

It was one thing to ask Nora to watch his dog a few times a week. She insisted. He reciprocated by caring for her yard, but to ask her eighty-year-old boyfriend? Sure, he was young at heart, but...

Ellis added, "Reka might cheer her spirits. We'll keep an eye on her for you. I'll take her on my daily walk, too. My old bones still need to get ten-thousand steps in. Come on in, Reka." He bent to meet the dog. She wagged her tail madly and scurried inside.

"Okay, but I owe you."

"I have beastly hedges that could use a trim," Ellis said with a twinkle in his dark brown eyes.

"You've got it. Cheers. Her food is—"

Ellis waved a hand. "Not a problem. Nora will tell me."

"Is she okay?"

"Aww, she'll be fine. I insisted she get the flu vaccine, especially with this virulent strain this year—saw it on the news, it's a nasty one—but, well, you know how she is. She didn't."

"Yeah. I'll bring soup back later for her." With a nod goodbye, he made his way to the inn.

He parked his Jeep and strolled to the porch with thermoses of tea and oatmeal.

Tasks piled in his brain. All his bosses were patient souls. Bookstore this afternoon. No inn tonight.

He had yet to text Charlotte. A surprise visit sounded crazy, overly eager, but he'd felt the spark between them while she was at his place. He had told her he'd text this morning.

He'd had trouble falling asleep last night—a surprise, given how he usually passed right out. He kept imagining what it would be like to kiss those pink lips or run his hands through her unruly hair. Or do more.

He found himself desiring one thing only, to snuggle next to Charlotte. If something serious came from it, then what? Not that anything serious came about from his flirtations.

But...

Dammit, he liked her. He had to seize the moment. Besides, she had to return to Boston in a few days. He glanced at his cell phone. It was seven thirty a.m. Good enough.

He texted her.

> Ready to show me your technical skills?

She responded with a smile emoji.

> Sure. Where should we meet?

> On the porch. I've got breakfast.

The next response took a moment. Had he over-stepped?

Finally, she responded, while his heart was in his throat.

> Be right down.

> Dress warm.

> Okay.

He stamped his feet, shivering with the morning's temperature drop. The sun would soon envelop the earth. It was in the low forties, back to the usual spring cold, and likely it would dip more this week.

Was he being too forward? She'd specifically said she didn't want "this," yet here he was, a mate showing up with food, foolish mug on his face, and thoughts he should chastise. Though she hid it under her layers of fleece and vest, he'd gathered a decent idea about the delicate bows of collarbone and shoulder, the lovely swell of her breasts, and he'd already seen the round curve of her rump while trekking on the path yesterday.

Alone...in the woods...the things he wished he could do with her. He blotted the thought or else he'd have trouble.

She strolled out, yawning but bright-eyed, and clad in thicker layers of jacket over a high-zipper fleece. He'd have to picture the fine skin beneath it. Maybe she'd sweat and would need to shed a layer or two.

Her erratic hair poked out from beneath a navy-blue ski cap. The morning sun brought out her attractiveness. A part of him wished to pull that cap off and caress the chestnut waves.

"Morning," she said with a smile.

"Ata mārie. Morning." He cleared his throat. "I brought breakfast." He lifted the thermoses.

She crinkled a brow.

"Don't eat breakfast?"

"Sometimes."

"What about dinner?" he asked as they turned the corner to his Jeep.

"Sometimes."

Something was definitely off with her today. Had he pressed his luck by asking her out again? He couldn't forget the touch of his hand upon her knee...and her reciprocated hand entwined with his. He'd seen her visibly fighting the attraction between them, too. Was this the indecision he felt coming off her?

"Don't see you much at the Millstone's dining room."

She didn't respond.

"Perhaps I could make you a real Māori dinner? I'm off tonight and tomorrow."

"I have plans with Veronica tonight."

"Tomorrow?"

She chewed her lip but then nodded. "Maybe?"

He opened her door to let her in. Cripes, was this 1950? Some women didn't like that. Who was he to fight against his mother's teachings though? She hopped in, and he closed the door behind her. There was a chance of a passing rain shower, so he had the hardtop on today. He hoped it would hold off. The waterfall climb would be slippery enough.

He got in and handed her a thermos. "I only have the one tea. You can have it." He reached into the cup holder and splayed two spoons. "We'll share the oatmeal."

Puzzlement filled her face. "Don't worry, I'm well."

She raised a thin, brown eyebrow over rich hazel eyes. "I wasn't implying—"

"Teasing, Charlotte. Drink and eat. I'll have some once you're finished. Though there are cases of flu going around."

"I'm all set. I always carry my hand sanitizer. And I'm a bit neurotic about washing my hands. Many years around kids means I take extra precautions."

"I forgot to get the vaccine this fall. My hands are always in muck or dishes at the inn, so I've got weathered soap hands. No need for sanitizer." He lifted a bruised and calloused hand. "Hope I don't catch this flu. Heard it's wicked."

"Wicked. Well, you do talk like a New Englander, too," she jested. She held out her hands. "Teacher's hands. I work in a germ factory. I got my flu shot, take my vitamins."

He couldn't resist. He laid his hand atop her smooth palm. Her touch was electrifying.

"So...you mentioned technical skills?"

"No worries. I'll have you."

"Where are we going?" Her gaze drifted around outside as he drove.

He turned down a road away from Summit Road toward the peaks. She kept her stare focused out her window and away from the mountains to their left. She took a hearty swig of the tea with a throaty moan that reminded him of other pleasures.

"This is flavorful with a hint of something I can't pinpoint. Same as you made for me yesterday?"

"Only the best for you."

"So...where are we heading?"

"A surprise."

"I'm not a fan of surprises."

He tried to smile broader to settle her nerves. "You like water, eh?"

"Yeah."

"That's your hint."

"I like to be prepared."

He squeezed her knee. He couldn't help himself today. "Live on the edge a bit. Some adventure?"

Her knee trembled beneath his hand. "I don't do adventure anymore."

"Anymore?" He really needed to know what the heck was with that and her "used to."

She dropped the tea thermos into a cup holder and turned toward the window, away from him as they whizzed past fields and meadows.

Something had happened to her. But what? He wished she'd tell him.

She was silent.

He chugged from the tea thermos. "Do you mind opening the oatmeal? I'll be a hungus soon if I don't eat."

"Sure." She did and handed him a spoon. "Hungus is like our hangry?"

He scooped mouthfuls in while balancing the wheel with a knee. "Exactly." He'd had this method memorized with all the shuffling between work shifts.

Belatedly, she asked, "Where's Reka?"

"With Mrs. Wakefield. This is not her sort of—" He caught himself before saying climb or adventure. "—thing."

Weaving along country roads, he made his way to the trailhead.

Her expression remained distant, troubled. "She'll be right," he said again.

"Huh?" Anxiety flickered in her eyes.

"*It* will be all right is what you say. Sorry, Kiwi slang. Hard habit to break. Nobody here speaks Kiwi."

"That must feel lonely."

He shrugged. "I call Kura every few days. We text a lot. I get my dose of Kiwi from her."

Her face softened. "I understand. Feeling lonely, away from your family."

Oh Charlotte, if you only knew. Maybe you do know. You make me feel less lonely. He refrained from asking about her family, as that might be her sore spot.

"No boots today?" she asked as they exited at the wooded railhead. He took another sip of the tea and offered it to her. She gulped. Her lips puckered. "You hid a lemon in there. That's what tasted different."

"Yup."

"Nice twist," she said wryly.

He slid a hand into hers—again. "My surprise. It has water and a smidge of a climb."

She turned to him, her face ashen. "I don't climb, Matiu."

He cupped her chin with his hand, his own pulse quickening. That strained crinkle in the middle of her forehead nearly broke his resolve. He wanted to kiss her worries—whatever they were—away. "I've got you. You love the outdoors, travel to some of the best locales for adventure, yet you don't tramp on mountains or climb? What happened? You told me you don't do it anymore. Can I ask why? I want you to be comfortable. I won't make you do this."

She averted her gaze. He dropped his hand. Charlotte needed a blanket around her, not a passionate kiss. She took his hand in hers.

Tears bubbled in the corners of her eyes. "I prefer to not talk about it, okay?"

"Okay." He took a deep breath and pointed to the tree line. "It's a quick walk in the woods, then short climb along a waterfall. I have harnesses, gear, all that. The view from the top is worth it. Let's have a go. But...you say the word, and we can turn back."

She sniffled.

Don't flee, don't flee. He wanted to assuage her distress.

"A waterfall?" she asked.

"You like water."

She held his gaze.

"It's a bridal veil waterfall. People cliff jump from the shorter waterfall beside it. I prefer a climb alongside the falls to the top of the taller one. There are no hiking trails to the top. I'll be with you the whole way." Her hand warmed in his. "I'll catch you."

"But kiwis don't fly."

He laughed lightly with her reference to New Zealand's iconic flightless bird...and the name they adopted for themselves. There was her sweetness. "You're well read. I can't fly, but I have mad skills."

She heaved a sigh. "Okay, I'll try."

"Sweet as. You'll let me know if you're feeling crook."

She muffled a laugh. The cloud on her face dissolved like an amber sun breaking a stormy dawn. "You have *got* to write these phrases down for me."

"Will do."

Thirteen

Charlotte stepped into the harness with feet clad in versatile pitch-climbing shoes provided by Matiu. For being a disorganized mess and overcommitted worker, Matiu was serious when it came to gear and outdoors stuff. He had it all in the back of his Jeep. *Or sprawled on his apartment floor*, she thought with a smile. Not strangely, it heightened her attraction to him.

Sure, his friendliness was one thing. The dimples, a bonus. He was a man who seemed to guzzle the outdoors like a thirst-quenching drink—the way she used to. And he was *nice*. It had been far too long since a man was just nice to her. Not a guy looking for a quick time.

Although she could lift the straps, her hands quaked, and she fidgeted with the helmet that had replaced her winter cap. The harness puddled around her feet.

"Here." Matiu slid the harness up, his hands gliding over her hips. He tightened each strap around her legs and waist, his body intimately close, his nearness breathable. "Have you done this before?"

"Ummm…" Her mind spun to join the riot whirling in her stomach. It was mostly from fear. The fear of climbing. The fear of plunging to her death. The fear of trying something adventurous when that exact thing had killed her sister. It was more than the climb though. It was also the fear of falling…for Matiu.

She inhaled him, trying by some magical force to consume his optimism and ambition…and free spirit. He smelled *good.*

"Climbing, I mean. I should have asked earlier. I was too eager to surprise you."

Was he blushing? A lock of dark hair fell against his eyes as he looked away toward the waterfalls, trying to cover his awkwardness.

"Once. In the White Mountains with my sister, Julie, on a ropes course. We zip-lined, too. Even with my fear of heights. All the lines were anchored…no trad climbing or any hardcore stuff." There, she said her sister's name aloud. Julie wasn't a ghost or memory of the past that never happened. She existed. She had been real.

"All good. This is a similar system. We designed this so guided groups can climb the rock face to the top of the waterfall. The trail keeps getting washed out for trampers, so the best route is climbing until the US Forest Service creates an alternate trail." He gestured toward the rock wall. "We already have fixed bolts. It's only sixty feet, but fun for beginners. There are two pitches with belays, and a ledge there," he said, pointing halfway. "Simple. It's not like free climbing El Capitan. We'll traverse right, reach the ledge, and cross left, then straight up. I'll take the lead. You climb behind me."

She released an "ah," appreciating his Yosemite climbing reference, though people *did* die on that monolith.

Sean had never enjoyed the outdoors. His idea of going outdoors was a booze cruise. He'd never once gone on the local paths around Boston with her. Bitterness swelled her memory.

She settled her hands on her waist. Matiu's hands were still there. She could almost lean in and kiss him. "I've got it."

He traced a finger over her wrist on the infinity tattoo. "Nice."

"Thanks."

"Maybe I'll show you mine."

She was blushing now. It was crisp outside, and hopefully he would think her cheeks were rosy from the cold, not his words.

"I can do this." It was more for herself than for Matiu.

He surprised her with a peck on her cheek. His lips were cool, the kiss too brief. He pulled back, tapped a hand on her helmet, and said, "You can. Let's review in case."

"In case?"

There were his dimples. "You have nothing to do but climb, but it's prudent to show your follower what's what."

They reached the rock wall. She watched him and followed his guidance as his hands moved with ease.

"Autoblocking will make it easier. You've done all this before?"

She nodded. He listed the steps, but her mind buzzed, and she tuned his words out. She had memorized all this before from her previous climb. Julie had been the leader. Her sister possessed admirable skills. She'd eaten the outdoors for breakfast. But Julie was gone.

Boldly, Charlotte stepped forward and repeated the steps with the rope, belay, and carabiner, her fingers not hesitating. "Like this?"

He laid his hands over hers and corrected one of her rope adjustments. "This is better."

She nodded, taking it all in. On top of being hyper-organized, she was a quick learner.

"I don't need to teach you a thing," he said, his voice smooth like gourmet hot chocolate.

She wished he'd stop touching her.

Nix that.

She wished he would touch her more.

The first scramble was over easy rocks with plenty of handholds. *Don't look down, don't look down.* She looked up. His well-defined calves, as he wore shorts today despite the temperature, guided her.

Don't stare at his butt.

So much for that. It was a fine one at that.

Winded, she reached the ledge shortly after him. They switched belays and continued the second pitch. Her thoughts for once—*my God, for once*—were not on her fears, her broken heart, her guilt, or her lost life. The waterfall hurtled over the ledge about twenty feet to their right and splashed down a narrow chimney, sending mist across her face. She inhaled the fresh scent of water and pine.

At the top, she welcomed Matiu's hand and stood with his help.

"That was amazing!" She exhaled exhilaration.

Matiu must have felt the high, too, for he scooped his arm around her waist and brought his face to hers. He angled right and planted a kiss on her lips, being sure to not clunk helmets with her. She reciprocated. His lips were sweaty, hot, and delicious.

She turned her body completely, facing him, her hips pressed against his upper thighs. She brought her hands to his lean, muscular back. Sweat moistened his T-shirt down the middle.

She lost herself in the kiss. For a long, soulful moment, she lost the broken woman inside.

Matiu hated that he had to work the evening shift at the bookstore. He craved more time with Charlotte. He drove them on a roundabout way to town, taking her past meadows and old rock walls, past red barns and through covered bridges. "This field," he said with a point to the left, "is full of wildflowers by midsummer."

She nodded and said, "Nice." She was glowing.

He was sure it wasn't from their kiss alone. He hated to ask questions that would spoil the mood, but he had to. "Charlotte?"

"Yeah?" She took a sip from her water bottle.

He paused, swallowed, and tapped two fingers on the steering wheel. "Can I ask now?"

Her eyes held him. He could read it in her expression—that she expected the next question—but her look was filled with permission.

"Why don't you go on mountains?"

She swiped at invisible hair on her face. "Five years ago, my sister was...uh, she died."

"I'm sorry." He squeezed her knee. To his relief, she clasped his hand.

"She and I were supposed to go to Chile on a challenging trail, the W trek, in Torres del Paine—anyway, I couldn't make it. My...," she said, faltering, pain crinkling her brow, an old scar ridged in the middle of her forehead growing deeper. He had determined it was a scar of sorts, not a laugh line or wrinkle.

"You don't need to tell me. I'm sorry. I shouldn't have pried."

Her words streamed. "No, no, I can. I want to. I was married before. My ex was an asshole. He controlled me. Everything I did. He hated to travel or to let me go places without him, but Jules and I had been hikers all our lives. We used to travel with our dad, but as we got older, in our twenties, we ventured on our own. Chile was supposed to be our first big trip five years ago. Nothing too technical, but an adventure."

He nodded.

"Sean pulled the plug last minute. Ironic since he was always going places for *work*." Her face crumpled, tears pooling in the corners of her eyes.

Matiu's heart ached with that punch. He had done this. He needed to undo it. "Don't. It's okay. Oh, Charlotte."

"I need to. It's so easy to share with you. It's like you get me. That sounds crazy, since we just met." She waved a hand, then skimmed her fingers to the edge of her long shirt, playing with it, folding and unfolding. Her intense focus was no longer on him. "Anyway, Sean was screwing around on me. It's mostly why we divorced. And the controlling thing. I didn't know then, before the canned trip with Julie. Anyway. I was supposed to go, and I didn't, and Julie is now dead."

"I'm sorry."

"Me, too." She sniffed.

She withdrew a tissue from her vest. She blew her nose. "Julie's body was never found. She died on the mountain."

Ah, hell. No wonder.

"Tomorrow is the anniversary of her passing...or of her having gone missing."

His pulse soared. "My God, I'm a prick. Sorry."

Her eyes were wet, but she turned to him, stalwart. "Nothing to be sorry about. You didn't do anything wrong."

"That took a lot to share. Thank you for trusting me."

His arms itched to pull her in close, kiss her so that she'd forget it all. He drove slower in town, delaying their parting. Work always called. He parked in front of the inn.

She leaned in and gave him a peck on his cheek as she departed. "Thanks for the climb. Thanks for listening."

"Tea tonight?" he asked, his heart so filled with hope it might burst.

She hesitated. "Sure."

Matiu slogged through his work at the bookstore and ate dinner alone. There was no dinner tonight at the inn, but Nate was fine with him using the kitchen to prepare tea at nine p.m. He went to the porch, tea in hand, heart eager to see Charlotte.

She wasn't there. He checked his phone. It was her usual time he'd figured out, when she'd already be outside. Charlotte seemed a creature of habit. It was colder tonight, but that hadn't stopped her before. He knew better than visiting her room again. Not at night, not when he was technically an employee. The other time had been an exception.

He texted her. No response.

Again.

Crickets.

How had he turned the first good thing that had happened to him in ages into a bit of a problem? The first woman who'd come along who opened his heart to something amazing...

He bottled the thought, dumped the cold teas on the front lawn an hour later and went inside to clean and go home. Maybe she just needed some time to herself.

Fourteen

The next day passed slowly, the way gumboots moved in mud. Everything Matiu tried, he failed. He tried texting Charlotte while on his morning shift at North Sports. It was too cold to do much trail cleaning with the ground frozen, and so far, no emergencies had come from the Middlesex Barracks via Commander Bixler.

No answer.

He called Charlotte again.

No answer.

He texted again.

Nothing.

He groaned, discouraged, but not fully giving up.

He couldn't barge in on her, though he bet his shoes she was probably hiding in her room. He purposely stopped by the inn on his day off in the hopes he'd see her or maybe catch her friend Veronica. Nothing.

He went home at lunchtime, disheartened and wondering what he had done wrong.

Today was the anniversary of her sister's death. Perhaps she just needed space to be alone, to grieve.

Kura had texted in the morning at six a.m., which was her ten p.m., probably after her hospital shift.

> Got great news on the location you wanted.

> Oh?

Lightness bloomed in his chest. That location near Queenstown was perfect for his shop.

> Call me later? You need to make a move on it fast. He won't hold it long.

> Okay.

Why did that "okay" not feel okay?

> Emailing the paperwork in a few.

> I'll call later. Sleep well, cuz. Talk to you soon.

His mood curdled as the excitement of her news wore off. He needed to sign the lease pronto. Kura's health was not improving. He'd done heaps of research on the latest medicine and treatments for multiple sclerosis. Being a nurse, Kura was educated in her options, too.

There was no cure, but they could do whatever possible to make her comfortable. He had located a hospital in Wellington that offered cutting-edge treatment. He needed to get home to New Zealand. He needed to support her in any way he could. Even if it just meant watching Jacob when she needed it. Though Queenstown and Wellington were on different islands, worlds apart, it was still closer than he was now.

He trudged up his steps after a quick stop to collect Reka at noon. Ellis was with Nora, and she wasn't doing poorly, but like most flu cases, hers was going to take a week or two to recover from, maybe longer given her age. He had dropped off Nate's signature chicken soup for her and a split pea and ham soup for Ellis.

This week, if the snow held off, he'd get to work in her yard. Soon, he'd be gone. He wished he could do more. He flopped on the couch, and a wheeze rattled his chest. He felt winded. *Nope, not the flu coming.* He willed it away. Just fatigue.

He opened his email to find the lease paperwork from Kura. He printed it and put it in his binder, then he left to shop in Waterbury. He had today off at the bookstore and inn. He liked to call Mondays his R&R days, only doing a morning shift at either the outfitter or with the forestry team, wherever he was needed. He'd usually spend the afternoon reading, researching, or off on a tramp somewhere, just him and Reka. He would've loved to spend that time with Charlotte.

Charlotte poured the milk in her tea. The white liquid mushroomed from the bottom like a cloud. She then twirled a spoon, causing the milk to swirl, a creamy storm within muddy waters. The milk lightened the tea as dairy met tea-infused water and then became an opaque solid.

She sipped it. "Meh." She placed the fine porcelain cup on a signature wildflower Millstone Inn saucer. It wasn't nearly as tasty as the tea Matiu had prepared for her. Despite being a habitual coffee drinker staying awake to grade papers and prepare lessons—and to avoid ghosts—she truly enjoyed the brew Matiu had prepared for her.

The bedside clock ticked. Noon.

Was she going to hide in her room all day? Her eyes had shed enough tears. They were puffy once again.

Every year, she did the same thing. She usually called out sick if the day didn't fall during April vacation, but often it did, or else it fell on a weekend. She was always alone to mourn. To beat herself up over all the mistakes. She'd call her mom and talk and cry. She'd visit an empty grave and place pansies by the headstone.

She recalled Veronica's attempt at a pick-me-up this morning.

"You've done all that a person can humanly do," she had said with a gigantic hug, a kiss, and then reluctant retreat to spend the day with Josh. Veronica had offered, more like pleaded, to take her to visit a maple syrup and sheep farm, but Charlotte declined. They had left without her—again. "I'll be back for dinner, and you better be out of your pajamas, okay?" were Veronica's last words.

As soon as she had shut the door, Charlotte crawled into bed. That had been at ten a.m. She stared at the tray loaded with hot tea, milk, fruit, and a scone. Thank goodness Matiu hadn't been on kitchen duty for breakfast. She could manage on this food all day. She itched to hit the media area to log online. However, she had seen Matiu's signature red Jeep Wrangler parked nearby earlier, so she shuttered that idea.

She glanced at her phone, rereading his texts. Then dialed her voicemail and listened to his message. Apologies. He'd done nothing wrong. She'd been a zombie of herself these past five years, floating through the daily grind, completing her work, staying under the radar. Getting by.

Matiu had reminded her of what she had been missing.

He was a breath of fresh air, fueling her soul. And it scared her.

She sipped the tea again, trying to enjoy it.

She *had* done all she could do to try to locate Julie. An annual ritual, she replayed it all in her head like a broken record. Charlotte had lied to Matiu when she said she hadn't been to South America.

When the news had arrived that her sister had gone missing, Charlotte, her brother Dylan, and their parents had flown to Santiago, Chile, to speak with officials. That had been a bust, so they flew to Puerto Natales and traveled north to Torres del Paine. Time was a factor. The longer Julie was unaccounted for, the less likely she'd be found. It reminded Charlotte of the stories she'd heard about missing children. The first twenty-four hours mattered. Especially in the harsh elements.

Charlotte relived those first moments countless times, analyzing for her own flaws, what they could have done differently. The scratched record kept spinning.

April was autumn in the southern hemisphere. Patagonia was notorious for wild winds and year-round snowstorms among its ragged, gray peaks that maxed in the 9,000-foot range. It was supposed to be the ultimate vacation. Charlotte had purchased a special camera lens for the trip, since autumn would be a rainbow of color, rivaling New England. Sean hadn't been too happy about that pricy purchase. He'd rather spend his money on late nights drinking with his *coworkers*. The woman he had left her for had been a coworker he'd met in a different branch.

Why can't I have you both? He had the audacity to say that when the truth about his affair emerged.

Shut up, Sean. You're not allowed in this memory.

When her family arrived in Chile, after getting nowhere with officials, they had no idea where to go. They had hired Esteban, who was a civilian private investigator in Santiago. After a few false leads, five years later, they were still searching for answers.

Julie had been a free spirit. She had worked a handful of jobs to make ends meet, from interning on political campaigns to working the Peace Corps in Albania and Malawi. Urban Massachusetts had a higher cost of living, so Julie couch-surfed when she was in between boyfriends.

Trying to keep frugal and avoiding Sean's wrath, Charlotte and Julie had not booked an expensive tour option that took people on the famous W trek in Torres del Paine. Instead, they had been meticulous in their planning, down to the hostels—or *refugios*—tent campsites, the food, the gear. All of it.

Charlotte had a bin filled with maps, itinerary, everything. Julie's lemon-yellow parka. It was the only item found of hers in their search, tangled and muddy between boulders.

That bin was stowed in her closet, for that's where skeletons belonged.

This year she had finally dug out her DSLR camera and resumed her hobby of photography. Instead of glacial lakes and mountainous backdrops, she stayed local and stuck to meadows and wildflowers. Slowly, she emerged from the hovering shroud of grief. Oh, so slowly. It was all too comfortable to return to the darkness.

She had a separate notebook filled with all her contacts, search locations, possible leads. Tears rolled down her cheeks as she recalled her endless thumbing through the now tattered pages, seeking any clue she may have missed.

They had canvassed nearby villages, spoken to tour agencies and hostels, visited every place that had been on the well-planned itinerary. Her sister's trail had gone cold. All Charlotte had to go on was the report of an autumn snowstorm, which had stranded people all over the place. Julie had been among the missing.

Their hiking system wasn't like the United States, where hikers often logged in or gave notices to park rangers or hiker stations. People usually knew where to look for you here. Chile did not have the same level of organized search and rescue teams. When you entered the great Patagonia range, you were on your own.

Only God knew where Julie was. Or had been.

They'd checked with local authorities on crimes and abductions in the surrounding areas. Charlotte had taken a leave of absence for the rest of the year, spending all summer there. Nearly five months. Searching villages in the biting winter of the southern hemisphere.

Nothing. Not a damn thing.

While Charlotte had planned their trip, Julie excelled in other areas, like finding the best gear, or picking the right aptitude hikes for them...or befriending fellow hikers on their trips. Their W trek was designed to avoid technical climbs because neither was skilled enough to attempt the harder treks. With this info in hand, Julie had gone alone to Chile, without her older sister to care for her.

Had Julie changed her plans? Communication via phone or internet was spotty in Chile, but Charlotte had received a few messages before Julie set off. She had joined with another group of backpackers for the trek. Knowing her sister had been with a group relaxed her worry.

Then the damn snow had come in, catching hikers unaware.

Just like that, Julie had been erased from the map.

Fifteen

Charlotte slept on and off all day. She missed having television or music or the chatter of students or the busyness of her day to fill the void in her heart and to silence the craziness in her mind.

Her phone pinged again. Matiu.

She'd screwed that up. Big time.

A knock on her door drew her from bed. She prayed it wasn't him. He couldn't see her this way. She was a mess.

Veronica's gorgeous face was filled with chagrin. "You're still here?"

Josh wasn't with her.

"Shower and come downstairs. Please?"

"I can't." She returned to the bed and flopped upon it. Veronica followed her in. She paced. Charlotte waited for the tirade.

Her best friend turned, her features twisted. Crossing her arms, she tapped fingers on each elbow and clenched her jaw. "Charlie, she is gone. Mourning is one thing, but you can't live *every* day like you died on that mountain, too."

"Damn, Ronnie, don't hold back."

"Every year, you do this. My friend Charlotte MacGregor left me five years ago, and I want her back! Tell me I'm selfish. I don't care. Mourn, cry, yes, do all that. You cannot keep blaming yourself. Sean was an asshole with a puny dick who did this to you. Move past it. If you want to blame someone, blame him! Throw it all his way. Not the healthiest way to cope, but anything is better than this. You are hot stuff. A great human being. Phenom. I know a guy who is interested in you beyond some fling."

"You don't know that."

Veronica exhaled loudly. "You won't know if you don't try!"

Charlotte curled her bare toes, digging them into the thick, braided rug at her feet. She couldn't hold her friend's gaze. Veronica's words were claws upon her skin, a scratching on her soul. She gritted her teeth, her jaw aching.

"And—" Veronica kept with her diatribe.

Charlotte waved a hand. "Enough! I get it!"

Veronica sat next to her. "I can't keep trying to make you happy. That's up to you. I miss you, Charlie girl."

Charlotte sniffed. "I miss you, too. I'm sorry I've been—"

"No sorry. You lost a part of you on that mountain. Sometimes being a survivor is harder. I get it. I don't talk about Mom anymore because it's been a long time, but I miss her. I can't let it destroy me. She's watching out for me," Veronica said, the ire in her voice replaced by her own anguish.

Charlotte cringed at her own selfishness. Veronica lost her mother to terminal cancer about ten years ago.

"Mom never met Josh, never saw me graduate from college, nor will she see my children when I have them. She will always be with me though. As Julie will always be with you."

They sat in silence, and Charlotte sobbed onto Veronica's shoulder.

"I need to live again," she said.

Veronica rubbed her back. "Yes, you do." She swiped at her own tears. "Shower. There is a guy looking for you. I saw him poking around earlier. Find him. He told me to tell you that he wants to make you dinner. He is off work tonight. Go to him. Have fun and see what happens. You must move past Sean. You must move past the guilt of Julie."

Charlotte nodded, trying to tell her brain those words.

"Love you," Veronica said.

"Love you, too." With that, her friend left.

Charlotte pulled her phone out of her purse. She had muted it after the last ping. Two texts from Matiu.

> I'm off today. Can I visit? Dinner?

> I'm an idiot. Please? Can I at least talk to you?

Instead of texting, she pulled on her shoes.

Matiu made his way to his apartment, arms filled with items he'd purchased from the gourmet store in Waterbury to make a signature meal—for one, since Charlotte was unresponsive.

He called Kura, lodging his phone between ear and shoulder while he carried the bags from his Jeep.

"Hey, cuz," he said to Kura. "How are you feeling?"

"Cruddy, but you got my email with the contract? Excellent news, right?" She yawned on the other end, clearly having just woken up. After all the years, it got cumbersome keeping his and her time straight. Soon, it would be a worry no longer.

"Sweet as," he said, though it held less enthusiasm than usual.

"Yes! The owner is ready to sign, but the lease starts in May, or else no deal."

"I saw. I already printed it." That meant he had to leave sooner—in a few weeks. Without questioning it, he said, "I'll forward money to your account for the down payment. Also, I have extra for you."

"I can't bludge off you."

"I'm not going to argue about it. We'll see you right. I'll be there for you and Jacob."

She sighed heavily on the other end. "You're stubborn."

"So are you," he said with a smile she couldn't see.

She said, "I'll handle the paperwork."

"Chur, cuz."

"It's the least I can do." Changing subjects, she asked, "How is everything there? Got loose ends to tie up?"

He dug in his pockets for his keys as he crossed the yard to the rear entrance of his apartment. "Nah, yeah, I met somebody."

"Oh." He could feel her animation. "Tell me!"

"She's choice."

She released a moan. "Not one to elaborate, are you? Does she know you're leaving?"

"Not yet."

"You need to tell her."

"I will. I'm gutted. Bloody awful timing, eh?"

She responded, "Life always has a way of doing that. Tell her. Maybe you two can make it work."

"Sixteen hours' time difference and eighteen hours of flying?"

"Maybe."

Reka barked from above, inside. "Gotta go. My sweet girl beckons."

"Which one?" Kura asked coyly.

"Funny."

She laughed, deeper.

It made his heart warm to hear her laugh. He missed her presence. He missed the comfort of *home*. "Talk soon. I'll scan the papers and email them tonight," he said.

"*Kia ora*, cuz."

"*Kia ora*," he said, bouncing the phone into his free hand to swipe the conversation off.

He turned to see Charlotte sitting on the steps. Cripes, how much of that had she heard?

"Hi," she said, quietly.

"Hi." He assessed her. She didn't appear on edge.

Maybe she hadn't heard much of the conversation. He had to tell her. Soon.

"Reka's going crazy with me sitting here."

"Then let's go inside, eh?"

She nodded. "Here," she said, grabbing a bag from him.

He repositioned another bag so he could unlock his door.

"Is that dinner offer still available?"

"Sure is."

"Great, and...I..." She shut the door behind her. Reka happily padded around her.

He dropped the bags onto the kitchen counter and returned to her. "I'm sorry. I pushed you. I asked too many questions."

She stopped him with a kiss. He gladly reciprocated, her lips tasting like tea and honey. Their kiss on the waterfall had been delicate, enjoyable. This one was harder, passionate. Would it be inappropriate to carry her to his bed right now?

He broke the kiss. "My situation is complicated."

"So's mine."

She tilted her chin up, and he stared at her awaiting eyes. It was his chance. Instead, he took her all in, every part of her. Her wild hair, her deep, soulful eyes, her alluring smile, her arms wrapped around his waist.

"Help me forget," she whisper-breathed upon his neck.

Goosebumps rose on his skin. "How about I help you remember instead?" He kissed her, refusing to let her go tonight.

Sixteen

The wind increased outside as Charlotte helped Matiu make their dinner. She chopped and listened to his explanations with rapt attention. "I guess our warm streak is over," she said.

"*Brrr.* Back to usual New England spring."

"Ha, what spring?"

"Exactly. The warmth teases us, but not until May or June some years do we enjoy it, and by then it's the heat of summer." He scuffled past her, his hand grazing her back purposely.

"Our autumns are pleasant. Winter is unbearable. Six months of icy and cold yuckiness."

He floated around the compact kitchen like a well-oiled machine. He nosed in the fridge. "Ideal for skiing."

"I don't ski. I've snowshoed, if that counts. Trail to a frozen waterfall. Tough, but worth it," she said.

"Sweet as," he said with a full grin. "I don't ski, either. I tried snowboarding a few times with friends but fell down more than I was upright. I work on the slopes in winter, but that's it. I'd rather tramp about."

She smiled. She was comfortable being in the kitchen with him, surprising herself.

"You've heard of a *hangi*?"

She nodded. "Cooking outside, in the ground, using the earth as your oven. I love that idea."

He grabbed ingredients and searched in cabinets for dishes. "Traditionally, Māori never cooked in their homes. They would use cooking sheds or cook outside. Modern lifestyle calls for modern changes, but I try to stay close to the recipes my mum taught me." He put a bowl on the counter.

"The *hangi* is symbolic, too, right?"

"Yup. The foods in a *hangi* all have special meaning and come from the gods. The kumara, our sweet potato, which is nothing like your yams, comes from Rongo. The vegetables are a gift from Haumia, and the fish from Tangaroa. The firewood, water, and earth all have origins in the gods, as well."

"Fascinating." She enjoyed his tours of both nature and culture and cataloged the information in her brain.

He held a potato. "These are the closest I can find to kumara like at home. They can be diverse in New Zealand. Nate recommended a place in Waterbury that has a variety of foods from Asia and Australia. My mum sends me stuff from the West Coast sometimes, too. Better variety there, and closer to New Zealand."

She nodded and rested the knife, done with chopping.

"So, you don't eat much, but do you cook?" he asked.

"Not much, but I'm learning. I know, late in life. Sean, my ex, used to tease me that I burn water." *Wouldn't let me cook*, was more like it.

"He was a jerk who didn't know what he had."

"With that viewpoint, you'd get on well with Veronica." She chewed her lip, refraining from saying her usual self-loathing phrase. She *was* a fine catch. It was Sean's loss. Not hers. The only mistake she had made was not seeing him for who he truly was and leaving him sooner.

He gurgled a snort. "I've already run into her. Not a woman I want to mess with."

"She could kick your butt with her designer shoes."

He chuckled. "I have no doubt." He unwrapped a nearby loaf. "This is rewena bread. It can be made in the *hangi* earth hole, but since I live in Vermont where the earth is frozen half the year, I make it in my own oven."

He broke off a piece and fed her. "Yum! But I can feed myself."

"Since you never make it to dinner at the inn, I wanted to be sure you ate."

She rolled her eyes.

"The bread has a flour and potato base. It takes a few days of feeding the starter—sometimes called the bug—before it's ready. Kind of like sourdough. No yeast is involved in it. It all starts with a potato and some sugar."

She snatched another piece, famished. "I once tried a sourdough with my science class. We named the starter Fred."

They both laughed.

He pointed to the other ingredients: fish, coconut milk, tomatoes, green onions, and lemons.

"I hope you're okay with fish."

"I live near Boston. Lots of fish. I've gotten used to it."

"I got snapper. Another tradition. Usually served raw, but I prefer it to be broiled. It takes an hour to marinate. Let's put that together first. It would be better overnight, but I need to feed you."

"You're off tonight?" It was a pointless question.

Charlotte, don't be a dork.

"Yup, you have me the whole night."

The nerves that had unwound with their kiss now bundled within her stomach. She took a steady breath. Matiu didn't bite. He was a gentle soul.

She found herself surfacing from her gloom as they talked and prepared. Following instructions was her forte, and cooking wasn't as hard as she'd once thought. "My mom always says that baking is science, and cooking is art. So, baking has always been more my thing. Give me exact measurements and instructions, and I'm good."

"Sweet as. It's your science brain."

She nodded. "Hey, so...I had a question?"

"Yes?"

"Those two women on the porch. What was that about?"

"Nothing. Not with either. Is that what you're wondering? They were tourists looking for a fling."

"They'd mentioned a friend."

His shoulders slumped as he spun his spice rack. He turned to her, full honesty in his face. "Their friend was a one-time thing. I used to do that. Not on purpose. Women seek an escape. They want something...I dunno, different, I guess." Hurt welled in his eyes. "I've tried to find a nice woman. I want to get married, have kids." His sigh sounded as heavy as it must have felt. "Working four jobs makes that tough. Not to mention it's hard to find a serious partner when most of them are only here for a week or two. I'm busy much of the time anyway."

She slid her hand into his. "I'll make the time."

He squeezed. "You're a gem."

"So you say."

"You don't see who you are. Special." He cupped her chin and gave her a slow, luxurious kiss.

She drank it like someone who was parched and lost in the desert.

His words were sincere while his touches pulled on a well of something much deeper. Rushing hot desire shot right down to her toes. Matiu said and did all the right things, and she knew in her heart, he didn't do this with everyone. He was a take him at face value sort of man.

He shifted around her and appeared with another mixing bowl. "Let's bake dessert while dinner marinates."

He placed the bowl in front of her. "Me?"

"You just said you love to bake, right?"

"This reminds me of a story Julie once told me. When she was in the Peace Corps. She went on a date with a local guy—I forget which country—anyway, he invited her to his place for dinner. When she arrived, she was expected to cook it! Cultural thing she hadn't been aware of."

She laughed. He laughed. Oh my God, she was laughing on the day Julie died.

"Did she?"

"Did she what?"

"Cook it?"

She scratched her head, trying to hide the grief. "I don't remember. Funny, because my memory is sharp. Maybe

I've been trying to dampen the memories, to help me heal…"

He pulled her into an embrace but didn't kiss her. Instead, he leaned his forehead against hers and spoke softly. "We're supposed to remember those we've lost, Charlotte. Not forget."

She suppressed the ache that had begun to rise in her chest.

"There have to be many happy memories, too. It's not all bad. How it ended…yes, that had to be heart-breaking. It sounds like you and your sister had a great time with each other, right?"

"Is that how you and Kura are?"

He gathered the ingredients for the dessert: flour, oats, coconut flakes, sugar. "We're keen on each other. She is a sister to me. My blood." He pointed. "Can you mix those dry ingredients while I cook the sauce. Then we combine and bake. These are Anzac biscuits. It was either this or hokey pokey ice cream, but that can't compare to creemees."

She chuckled, imagining them doing the aptly named dance. "Hokey pokey ice cream?"

He shrugged, focused on his task. "Vanilla ice cream with honeycomb toffee bits. Sweet as. Reka loves it."

Reka's ears perked with her name being said, but she didn't open her eyes from her dog nap in the corner. She repositioned her head on her paws and kept snoozing.

"I made pavlova the other night at the inn. Did you try it?"

"Afraid not." She shifted on her feet, done with mixing the dry ingredients.

"So Anzac biscuits are cookies that have a longer shelf-life. They don't have eggs. During World War I, they were sent to the soldiers in the Australia New Zealand Army Corps overseas." He stirred the butter and corn syrup in the pot on the stove. "Anyway, you'd like Kura. She supported me through my rough teen years. Taught me to see the potential, weed out the bad influences. I was caught up with troublemakers."

"No, you?" she scoffed, playful.

He seemed bashful. He finished up the sauce. They combined the ingredients and then scooped rounded heaps of batter onto cookie sheets.

She squeezed his shoulder. A strong, well-defined shoulder. "She has a son?"

"Yeah, she's divorced. She also has advanced multiple sclerosis. There's a novel treatment she can try. There's no cure, but medicine is evolving."

"Oh, I'm sorry. Is that why you're going home to visit soon?"

He put dishes in the dishwasher. "Yeah. I've also been saving extra money for her."

She was spellbound. Matiu was the farthest thing from a player. So why was she fighting this? Long distance relationships could work. Boston and Vermont weren't too far from each other.

They finished their work in the kitchen, cleaning while the cookies baked. When the timer went off, he removed them from the oven to cool. He leaned over, rested a hand on her hip, and sniffed. She loved his closeness.

"You do know how to cook."

"Well, with your help. And this was baking, remember?"

"Want a tiki tour of my pad? All five hundred feet of it? We didn't have a lot of time last time you came over." He kept a hand upon her hip to guide her from the kitchen. "Okay, you met my couch and the clutter in here. I *am* a slob."

"You've said, but I sense a method to your madness."

He guided her to the bathroom. "Bog." He laughed at himself. "Loo. Or washroom or bathroom or whatever you all call it."

She cracked up. "Bog. *That* is a new one. I like it. I mean it. Teach me this lingo. I do enjoy it."

He ushered her to the living room. "Come to New Zealand to learn. With your photographic memory."

"I should."

"You met Dob." He patted the Dobsonian telescope. "Closet here...and then my bedroom, but that's a bigger mess," he said as they tripped over boxes, piles of papers, and a laundry basket.

She must have made a face.

"Hey, that's clean. Honest to G."

"Sure, it is." Boldly, she stepped into his bedroom, her pulse racing. It had been far too long since she had slept with anyone. "That fish has to marinate for a few hours?" She offered her best seductive look. Gosh, she was inept at this. Sean had always initiated with her. Always in control. Well, when he *wanted* to be with her. The last six months of their marriage had been sexless, loveless.

"Yup," Matiu said, eyes dreamy in the lower light of his bedroom. She was surprised to see a well-made bed. The mess was everywhere, but not the bed. She would bet it had clean sheets, too. He didn't cease to amaze her.

He held her close and kissed her. Tenderly, slowly. He cupped her chin as he drew back. "I've not done this in a while."

"Me, neither."

"It's cliché, but I have to say it." He licked his lips and admired her. They inched closer to the bed, his hands on her hips and her arms around his waist. She shivered with intimate proximity.

"Oh?"

"You're hot stuff."

She laughed, light-headed from fatigue and desire. "Isn't that what Americans say? Come on, I've picked up *some* American slang."

She swiped her hair, straightened her shirt, and fidgeted with her earrings. "I look horrid today. I was crying this morning." She smacked his chest. "That was not a Kiwi phrase. Definitely American."

"Why do American women always say they look bad?"

"Kiwis are different?"

"Not sure. I didn't date much before I moved here. The women I knew as a teen embraced their beauty."

"Hmm."

"Charlotte?"

She tipped her face toward him. She yearned for his lips upon hers again.

"Want a biscuit? I'm starved."

She smiled for real, the muscles on the sides of her face aching from it. "Sure."

They moved to the couch, and he brought a tray of the Anzac biscuits. "Tea?"

"Maybe later."

She moaned with a bite of the delicious coconut cookie. "Tea, biscuits. A whirlwind tour of New Zealand. I can't wait for the fish." Not realizing how hungry she was, she finished the cookie in three bites, licking her fingers.

He ate a second cookie. Crumbs stuck to the corner of his mouth. She wiggled closer to him, enjoying the shared space, and lifted her lips to meet his. "Crumbs," she whispered.

He pulled her in, his hand sliding lower down her back. She realized belatedly she was not wearing anything remotely sexy underneath. Matiu didn't seem like the kind of man who cared. At least she'd showered and shaved this morning.

His kiss grew deeper, as their tongues, sweetened with coconut and syrup, explored. He threaded his fingers through her hair, releasing a low moan as she slipped a hand inside the back of his jeans.

Breathless, she writhed. "Make me forget."

He corrected her. Again. "I'll help you remember."

Shivers of anticipation prickled her skin as he leaned her back on the couch, his body long and lean and firm against hers. His hand meandered beneath her shirt. She felt like a teenager. He cupped her breast and teased a nipple. "You're like heaven, Charlotte."

His saying her name brought her to a peak of wanting. She needed him.

He pulled her shirt off over her head. Well, the navy blue molded-cup bra wasn't unattractive. When was the last time she had purchased sexy undergarments?

"I bet you taste like heaven, too."

"I'm far from celestial," she said, self-conscious.

He kissed the tops of her breasts, sending ripples of pleasure through her entire body. He traced her neck and shoulder with dozens of kisses. His body pressed against her and her desire soared. The intuitive yearning returned like riding a bike. It had been far, far too long.

Her mind emptied, and she reciprocated, undressing him first by taking off his shirt. Then unbuttoning his jeans. He was hard against her, hands everywhere. She didn't just tingle from his touches, she downright shook.

"Do you have any protection?" She could not believe she was saying this. Sure, there had been a few unlucky men after Sean, but it had been so long, and with Sean she had been on the pill.

"Cripes! Yes! Be right back." He nibbled her bottom lip before untangling himself from her.

She missed his nearness immediately, almost irrationally.

He returned with a box of condoms from his bedroom. "Sure hope these aren't expired."

"Me, too."

He read the box. "Whew." He returned to kissing all her parts, her mind spinning at his affection.

He unzipped her jeans and pulled them off ever so slowly, his gaze not leaving her. Dark and deep. His sincerity put her insecurity at ease. The quakes settled, and she fell into the rhythm of touches and kisses.

The hint of his tattoo twisted around his shoulder and upper bicep. As she expected, he had a fine, chiseled torso.

Boldly, she leaned forward and kissed his chest, nipples, abdomen. He tasted salty from manual labor.

"I should have showered," he said, reading her mind.

She drew him harder to her. "Save that for the morning."

"You'll stay then?"

He angled his kiss lower, leaving invisible imprints on her breasts, stomach, and ohhh, he went farther. She lay back while his hands seared a path down her thighs. He swiped a gentle hand across her panties and—

"Oh," she said, her entire body trembling from the intimacy of his mouth on the core of her.

Far. Too. Long.

She probably enjoyed it too much, but screw it all, it was damn good. She hoped her moans of ecstasy didn't bother Mrs. Wakefield below.

He brought her to a roaring peak, her own personal summit. She had never been so aroused or pleasured by a partner. Matiu was passionate and considerate and thorough. She lost herself to all his kisses and touches as they made love on the couch. She panted, their bodies joined, tormented by the sensuous motion, enjoying every part of him.

It was both raw and sweet.

She exalted in the awakening within her.

She didn't think about the painful memory of today. She didn't think about the past. She thought only about the present and the enchanting soul intertwined with hers.

Seventeen

Matiu awoke in the middle of the night, craving her more. She was naked, curled within his arms, and his body responded with instinct. He traced a hand upon her arm, and she released a whimper as his touch fell upon her hip, then slid to the front across her taut lower abdomen.

He didn't expect her words. "What is this?"

"What, me bedding you?"

"That's a bit medieval. Besides, we were on the couch. Maybe we should call it what it is."

"It's more than sex." He kissed her shoulder, relishing her taste. He'd enjoyed kissing her entire body. He enjoyed having her in his bed. He squeezed her tighter. She squeaked.

He laughed. "You a mouse?"

She giggled, too. "Sometimes."

"You eat like one."

He realized they shared another commonality besides the ambition that comes with being a nature buff. They were both afraid of being abandoned. Her cuts went deep—her ex, her sister. His—maybe the slices were superficial. He was finished with flings that went nowhere. His longest relationship, a year, had ended in disaster.

Lynn had grown tired of his restless spirit, his over-commitments, and his bailing on her. His heart had been steadfast in that relationship. There was no doubt. Hers had not been. Maybe she had only stayed with him for his dog. Reka won people over.

Unlike Charlotte, he didn't know from where his commitment issues stemmed. Maybe it was the emptiness that sat in his soul—he sorely missed family, he missed *home*. He'd masked his feelings for so long, not exposing his vulnerability.

Charlotte lay still and quiet in his arms. He wondered what she was thinking. He was happy she'd stayed. It'd grown colder, and he saw a trace of snowflakes with his peek outside.

Was his poor track record with women his own doing? Had he created his own perceived prejudice against himself, not allowing a woman to get close to him? And if so, why?

Mindlessly, he stroked Charlotte's hip. Goosebumps rippled on the skin beneath his fingertips. Perhaps moving home would settle him once and for all. He could commit to one job, one woman.

That woman needed to be Charlotte.

It was foolish to fall so quickly, but he wanted to adore every inch of her. Wanted to bring her along on his dream venture. He settled his thoughts by sharing a story. "I told you I can help you remember."

She rolled to face him. He inhaled the fragrance of her hair. Her breath was minty fresh from borrowing a spare toothbrush. He caressed a finger along her round chin.

"What did you mean?" she asked. She stroked the *piko-rua* necklace he never took off.

"In the Māori culture, there are special ceremonies to remember the dead. A long time ago, Māori used to exhume the bodies, the bones, a year after their death and rebury them. In modern times, there are different traditions such as revealing the gravestone on the first anniversary." He hesitated on the next part and took a fearless breath. "Your sister, Julie, never had a funeral?"

Charlotte's face, hard to read in the darkness of the room, seemed to scrunch, but then she sighed. "No. We had a memorial service for her, but no body, no burial. An empty tomb with a gravestone."

He stroked her hair. "I'm sorry."

"Me, too."

"I wonder if the reason you've had difficulty with mourning and moving past is because...first I must say this, Charlotte. It's not your fault."

The dam retaining the tears broke, and she sobbed softly.

"It wasn't," he assured, touching her face. Charlotte's situation reminded him of Kura's. He could only do so much to help. Ultimately, it was out of his hands. He allowed Charlotte a moment. She calmed herself quickly.

He continued, "In our culture, if the spirits are not satisfied by a *tangi*, a funeral, the spirits may wander. The family members also undergo harder lamenting and stress."

She snuggled closer to him. "Julie's spirit may be wandering the earth?"

"Perhaps. It's not the Christian way to view it. Even if the earth in Chile has become her grave, she needs a proper funeral for her family to release her spirit. It's more for the family than for the lost loved one."

"I see."

He kissed her. "I don't say this to upset you. It's just one viewpoint."

"I understand. The remembering?"

"She will always be here," he said, placing a hand over her heart. It thumped madly beneath his palm. "You must release her spirit to the afterlife for you to be truly free."

"Why the one-year thing?"

"Some believe the dead watch over us. To pay homage a year later lets us remember them once more, then we can release them."

"Did your father have a *tangi*?"

He nodded. "A modified ceremony. He was *pakeha*, of European descent. His family wanted a traditional Christian funeral and burial. My mum's family also performed a *tangi* for him. I attended my father's church as a kid, too. Some people falsely believe that interfaith families raise confused kids. It's quite the contrary if done well. I've learned to appreciate both cultures and faiths, and my parents presented them in a nurturing, open way." He paused. "Faith aside, I do have a bit of restive personality. I wear a lot of hats."

"You're alive but an aimless spirit, too," she said languidly.

"I guess even the living can have their own restlessness, too."

They lay quietly for a while. Then, he spoke. "Charlotte?"

She cradled her head into the crook of his arm, her breathing growing heavy. She didn't respond.

"Come with me to New Zealand," he whispered, his own voice weak, breaking. "To live." He fingered his necklace. "Be my forever," he whispered.

She was already snoring.

"*Po mārie*, Charlotte."

Five a.m. came, and so did Matiu's arousal. He rolled over, happy to find Charlotte still in his bed. He kissed her cheek. She moaned and leaned into his body, aligning all their parts just right. They were already naked, but he needed a shower.

"Hi," he said.

"*Kia ora*," she returned. "Well, it's morning. *Ata mārie*."

He kissed her throat and allowed his hands to explore her body, landing upon and squeezing her bottom. She was thoroughly receptive as their kiss delved farther, deeper, beneath his blanket. A quick switch and she was straddled upon him, kissing his chest. The blanket fell off her shoulders and landed around her naked hips. "Tell me about your tattoo," she asked, nuzzling her lips against his torso.

"That tat doesn't have real meaning, not to me anyway. Got it when I was in a gang. Simple Māori design."

She stopped in her kisses and peered at him, her hair messy across her forehead. "A gang?" She rested her chin on his chest. Her breasts were lined well with his groin.

"Yup, part of the rebellious phase."

He stroked a thumb on her wrist. "Yours?"

"I got it with Julie after high school, long before she disappeared. We were very young. It's an infinity symbol. Bittersweet, I guess. That she'll always be with me."

"Did you go to Chile, after, I mean?"

"Yeah. We searched for five months. Not only was there no funeral, but we never got confirmation of her death. I know now. She's dead. Sometimes I imagine her alive, and the happy news coming through my email contact. That's a delusional fantasy. It's been five years."

He squeezed her hand. "It's okay to hope. It's also okay to mourn...and let go."

She rested her cheek on his abdomen, her hair draped across it, and her face warm on his skin. "And to remember." After a moment, she drew her kisses back to him.

"Charlotte...we don't have to. I gotta shower soon. Get ready for my shift."

"I want to. You're right. This is more than sex. You've helped me remember a lot of things..."

It was her turn to make love to him, as she rose and straddled him. His mind liquified. Her breasts were perfect even in the low light as she rocked her hips and they swayed in a deep rhythm. He moaned with the pleasure she unleashed. She was indeed a heavenly creature. He would cherish every moment with her, as long as he had her.

Eighteen

While Matiu was in the shower, Charlotte paced in the living room, wearing only his T-shirt and her undergarments. The wind roared against the windows, and she jumped at a loud gust. This apartment was on the upper floor of a house that had to be at least a hundred years old. Her steps creaked upon the floorboards.

She dreaded the drive home tomorrow.

She settled on the couch with the tea Matiu had already prepared for her. In place of a cry hangover from her annual mourning fest, she had the morning-after glow of a magical night of lovemaking. For the first time in years, she'd slept not only without her sleep aid, but well. Like, *well*.

She needed to gather an idea of where this relationship was heading. Perhaps they could make it work. Vermont wasn't too far from Boston. They could see each other on weekends and during her breaks.

While she waited to talk to him about her plans, she perused his stacks of magazines and whatnot on the coffee table.

She released an audible sigh after a sip of tea. Matiu had converted her. A longtime groupie to the local coffee houses in Boston, and now she was in love...with tea. She flipped through the magazines. All outdoors or nature topics.

Be still her heart. One cover showed two kayakers in the foreground of Mitre Peak. New Zealand was still on her bucket list. Perhaps she could muster the courage, manage the eighteen-hour flight, and visit him there? Maybe meet Kura, hang out, explore both islands? She daydreamed, her mind racing with an excitement she hadn't experienced in years.

The Tongariro Crossing had been high on her must-see list with its inspiring volcanoes, black rocks from ancient lava flow, and the shockingly teal Emerald Lakes. There were so many places to see. The Southern Alps, the Remarkables, Abel Tasman's sunbaked glistening shores alongside the ocean where she imagined kayaking with Matiu, the interesting Punakaiki rocks that looked like pancakes, and of course lupine and glaciers...

Though she had just purchased the travel guide at the bookstore, she'd already read a lot about the island nation they called Aotearoa. Eagerness percolated through her veins. The travel bug had nestled its way back into her heart thanks to Matiu. Maybe she would even travel with him to New Zealand at some point. It sounded like he visited home as often a he could.

The shower turned off.

She shifted her feet to stand and accidentally knocked a thick pile of magazines and papers off the table. Groaning, she set the tea on the table and got on her knees to gather the scattered papers. Her eyes caught the title on a binder that slipped out of the magazines: *Mana ao turoa: An Outfitter That Takes You Beyond.*

Within, she scanned a recently downloaded lease agreement with a Queenstown address, interior building designs, endless pages on gear from kayaks to backpacks, spreadsheet with cost projections and budget, and a vision statement page.

The lease had the date of May 1st of this year. With Matiu's name on it.

She blinked, slowly reconciling the words.

Matiu strode across the carpeted floor. "Hey, Charlotte, I was thinking—"

Her hands shook, and she slammed the binder shut and placed it on the table. She sat on the couch. "S-Sorry. The papers fell. I wasn't—wasn't snooping," she faltered, her pulse fitful, her throat dry, and her heart as heavy as a stone.

"I meant to tell you. It's okay, you can look at it."

"You're leaving? Like, for real leaving, not going to just visit family?" She hugged her arms to her trembling middle.

He was in a towel, wet, hovering near, smelling of lemongrass soap. He sat beside her, a hand outstretched. "It happened fast. The ideal location for my business has just opened. He needs the lease signed and returned for May. I-I meant to tell you. I just didn't know how."

"You're opening your own outfitter?"

"Yes. Come with me."

She gritted her teeth, abating the riot of questions she wanted to fling at him. "That's ridiculous. I can't go with you."

"But you...I...it's—"

Repeating his phrase from the night before she said, "It's complicated. I get it. This, *us*, should not have happened," she finished for him, wiggling away from his proximity.

"You don't mean that, do you?"

She fought against it all. She fought against the truth. She liked him. Maybe loved him, as lunatic-sounding as that was. No, this was not love. Fun, that was all. She quelled her pain and softened her voice. "It's your dream? To open an outfitter?"

He nodded. "I've been planning it for years. Saving every penny, and I'll be closer to Kura to help." He scuffed a hand on a cleanly shaven chin. "I should have told you."

That explained all his jobs, working himself to the bone. He wanted to leave.

"You're leaving."

Another person. Leaving. Could she not hold on to anything? Not one damn, good thing? Tears found their ways to her eyes. She wouldn't know if this *was* a good thing. Not with him gone.

"Oh, don't cry. *Come with me.*" He reached for her hand.

She shivered, uncontrollable spasms erupting from within. "This is stupid. Just a..." She fumbled her words.

He came closer, laid a hand on her knee. "No, it's not stupid," he said, firmly.

"I don't know. I don't know. I have so much here...my job..." she began and ended as abruptly. That was all she had. Well, Veronica, some friends, her family—but they all had their own lives. They had all moved on since Julie's death.

She had been the person stuck on pause. Maybe even going in reverse.

Stuck in mud. Like on these darn mountains.

She adored her students, but each year she had a fresh batch of kids to bond with, and each year she saw them off to the next grade. A teaching job might not be hard to acquire in New Zealand.

Matiu's phone beeped a few times, several texts coming in.

She jumped.

He moaned. "Not many have my phone number. Mostly work. SAR team. Family."

Me, she thought.

He got up and hurried to the plugged in cellphone on the counter. "Cripes, not good," he said, swiping and reading his screen.

He dialed. "Hey, mate. Got your messages. Fill me in."

Charlotte tried to listen while her mind processed everything they'd just discussed.

"Kelly and Neil are sick with the flu, too. Is Commander Bixler going to try the other teams? What about state police troopers?"

He paced the room, deftly weaving through the disorder. He nodded, though the person on the other end could not see. He kept a hand on the rolled towel edge around his hips. In the light, Charlotte had a much clearer view of his detailed tattoos that appeared more like an ancient script than symbolic Māori art.

"Will he call in a helo from the Guard?"

Matiu went to the window, drew a curtain back. "Windier there, too. You're breaking up, mate. Repeat?"

More listening.

"Reka and I can't do it alone. Jack's dogs aren't ready, and he's out of town. You're all sick." He paused, listened. "Right. I'll meet you at the trailhead?"

More nodding, his face filled with intensity, but it was also confident, competent, and ready for action.

He then turned to her, caught her gaze. His brown eyes grew wide, dark eyebrows lifted. "Okay, I'll meet you there."

Her lips had gone dry. She dug for her lip balm in her handbag. Not finding it, she dumped the contents, her hand sanitizer skittering across the countertop. She needed water. Her mind whirled.

"Charlotte?"

She turned, standing in front of him, still in his T-shirt that smelled like him, and he in a damp towel. "Yeah?"

"Let's get you back to the inn."

He tossed his phone to the couch. He darted into his room; she followed.

"What happened?"

"There are two stranded trampers on the mountain. The snow's not deep in town, just a dusting," he said with a flick of his chin toward the window. "But I bet there are six inches on the mountain."

She bounced a curled knuckle against her lubricated lips as he got dressed.

"All the SAR team is sick. That was Greg. He's got the flu, too. He took the call from VSP and will meet me at the trailhead. The commander's calling the helicopter crew." He sighed.

"There's more?"

"Usually, a couple state police troopers join us on the search, the whole unified command thing. They run the show. We're like, outsourced, ya know? However, the state police are occupied with a dicey accident on the highway, north. No local troopers to contact. Our team is down two, maybe three, people."

"Are the hikers injured?"

He shook his head as he dressed. "Not sure. They were hiking the Lincoln Peak track—the entire Long Trail is a sweet multi-week trek, takes you over numerous peaks, some four-thousand feet high...anyway, a couple got caught on the ridge with this storm. They're likely hypothermic, disoriented. We know roughly where they are. They're on the Gap-to-Gap section of the Long Trail, beyond the shelter and ski lift. It's a two-mile ascent, a thousand-foot elevation gain through woodland. We need to get to them, stabilize them, and wait for the helo."

He swallowed and paused in his explaining, as if going through something in his mind. "The helo crew then lowers a Stokes rescue stretcher—it's like a basket—and paramedic. There's a shelter where they could have sought cover, but they're no longer responding to texts. Phone communication and wireless ability is sketchy, but there is usually okay reception near the shelter and ski lift. We use radios with GPS and a location beacon."

She absorbed the information as he gathered spare socks and a T-shirt from his dresser. "You said Greg is sick and there are no other crews?"

"He's all we have. Our team is small for the area, only us four, plus a few assigned state police troopers. Some crews have seven or more people and a few dogs. The commander has tried reaching other teams without luck. Some key cell towers are down. He can keep trying with the radio. See if anyone can break away from that accident."

Beads of perspiration dotted his high forehead. He didn't look so hot either.

Nineteen

Matiu made his way to the inn. Only a dusting was on the ground in town. Just as he put the Jeep into park at the curb, his phone rang.

"Hi, Commander Bixler." Joaquin never called him, just Greg. This wasn't good. Matiu put the phone on speaker.

"Hi, Matiu. Greg's wife just called. He collapsed on his way. Seems his flu is worse than he let on. He won't be able to make it to the trailhead."

Matiu's pulse raced. "Is he okay? What next?"

Bixler's sigh was audible. "He'll probably be okay. She thinks he is dehydrated. She's taking him to the hospital. Several cell towers are disabled. I radioed the helo crew. They're set, but I can't get through to any other teams. The helo crew won't go until they are radioed with confirmation from the team. All manpower is dealing with that highway mess."

"What about Waterbury?" They were one of the best backcountry teams.

"No luck."

Charlotte was quiet beside him. Matiu gave her a long look. "Commander, I have an idea."

"Hit me."

"My friend is visiting from out of town. She's got back-country experience and first aid training. In fact, she co-ordinates first aid and emergency training for her school district in Massachusetts."

Joaquin was quiet for a moment, then said, gruffly, "She a volunteer? Got SAR training?"

It was his turn to pause. "Not exactly."

"You know procedure. My superiors would bite my head off if they got wind of this...especially if they heard an untrained civilian was accompanying you. What if something doesn't go well? No, we need to follow command procedure. Wait for more teams."

"I'm going."

"Not alone," he responded, tersely. "Matiu..."

He nibbled his lip, hearing the frustration in Joaquin's voice. He never pushed an authority before, not like this, and not the SAR commander. "I've got Reka."

He exhaled. "I'll keep calling around. You get to the trailhead and wait for an update. I can't, you know, well...," he rambled. He sounded bloody tired, too. Probably coming off an evening shift. He couldn't approve the order to go alone. If Matiu did, it was on his head.

"Got it. I'll check in." Extenuating circumstances called for pushing the rules.

"There has to be someone else," Charlotte said as soon as he disconnected.

"You can do this, Charlotte. You're skilled, I've seen it. A dedicated follower, a helper. You're sharp. You've got first aid expertise. And some states require less than we do for qualifications. They use whoever can get the job done." He was mostly trying to convince himself with his words. He hated to go against orders.

"There has to be someone else," she repeated, visibly shaking. "You'll get in trouble."

"There is nobody. You, Reka, and me. Reka is a skilled SAR dog and will do most of the work. We haven't finished clearing trails so there are also twigs, branches, and any trees that have fallen in winter. Add inches of snow to that. It's either a hardened mess or a sloppy mess. We won't carry anyone down on the Stokes stretcher unless it is our only option. That takes a four-man team. We find them, stabilize, call, trigger my location beacon, then signal the helicopter with flares to guide them to the location. Just need to get to them, Charlotte."

Silence. Dead silence.

He squeezed her hand. "I need your help. Can you tackle this mountain with me?" The only other option was to wait for more crew to arrive. If they arrive. By then it could be too late. He never lost a rescue.

She opened, then closed her mouth.

"It's just another hike, that's all. I could use a second hand, even if you're just spotting me. Plus, you have first aid training." He coughed. His throat scratched. *Nope, not sick. Not sick.*

Another painfully long silence. She said, "I have a heavy jacket in Veronica's car."

He took that as a yes.

The dusting in Winterwood was nothing compared to the several inches that met them on their drive to the trailhead. Matiu had the drive memorized. Through the covered bridge across the Mad River, several winding turns, a length on the main road, and then toward the App Gap.

When he turned onto the aptly named Summit Road, Charlotte released a muffled whimper. She rifled in her pocket for something. She withdrew lip balm and applied it. Tucked it away. Removed it again, reapplied.

"It will be all right, Charlotte. Breathe."

She nodded, decked in her own parka along with borrowed outer gear he grabbed from Kelly's extra stash at the fire station—snow pants, calf-high cold-weather boots suitable for mud and snow, and gloves. The temperature gauge read thirty-three degrees Fahrenheit. Topped with her navy-blue ski cap, she looked ready to conquer a mountain. Nerves aside, of course.

It was a several-mile drive up the steep road to the trailhead.

His stomach lurched and not from the road. He was used to the twisting turns. It was something else. All his mates had the flu. He had the chills, but he attributed it to the cold outside. He willed it away. He thought the shower this morning would have nipped those symptoms that had been bothering him since last night. Nope. Cripes.

Snow covered the road, but his Jeep was reliable, and he wouldn't require chains. They usually kept this road plowed in the winter. If they didn't, there would be no ski season. However, ski season was over. He stayed in low gear and took it easy. At least nothing appeared frozen on the road. Their tire marks blazed the path for all who might follow, not that any fool would drive up there today. The ski lifts were all shut down, officially on summer break until November.

Charlotte was silent, staring forward. The peaks were obscured in low clouds, and snowflakes fell with a splatter against his windshield.

Her quietness was unnerving. He had two options: let her ruminate or talk calmly with her. He wasn't sure which method would work to ease her fear. She seemed almost paralyzed by it. That could spell disaster. He'd only known her for a few days, but he guaranteed she would be an asset and see the mission to the end. Was he pushing her? He really needed her. "Are you okay with this?"

"Not sure yet. Ask me in a few minutes."

Reka barked from the back seat. "Ready, girl?" he asked. She barked again. She was already in her vest with her bell, the leash beside her. She tapped her tail on the seat. He had her treats in his pocket.

He took a profound breath like he always did for a search or rescue to get his mind in the right place. "Would you like the play-by-play?"

Charlotte slowly bobbed her head.

"We'll use the snowshoes to get to the shelter. Sounds like we may have about six inches up there, and I suspect the mud beneath is frozen. That helps. The path is purposely made for snowshoes. There's only one spot with an easy ladder pitch. A steady climb. No scrambles, no trad climbs, or anything with ropes. Greg takes his kids this way."

He meant that to ease her mind, but now it sounded condescending. "A bit under two miles to the shelter and clearing. It'll be windy at the trailhead, but once we're in the woods that won't be an issue until we reach the clearing. On a decent day, the wind can be rough. But I assure you, this end of the trail is easier."

Okay, the no-ropes thing wasn't a certainty either. It all depended on where he found this stranded couple. Most likely they wouldn't require the ropes, but he'd brought all the rescue gear in case. The lost souls could have slipped over a rocky edge, although the Long Trail in this part didn't have any nasty drops.

He mentally reviewed everything that was tucked carefully in his pack.

Helmet, goggles, leather gloves, water, food, ropes, carabiners, rappelling equipment, headlamp, extra clothes, compass, first aid kit, bivvy bag, stove, maps, markers and tape, shovel, hand-held radio and phone, personal location beacon, flares, pocketknife, ice axe, and crampons.

He repeated them to himself.

There was an emergency gurney stowed near the shelter if the helo couldn't lower the Stokes stretcher. They probably couldn't manage that in the snow, with just the two of them. The gurney required a four-person crew at least. He already wore his layered clothes down to neck and leg gaiters.

"Matiu?"

"Eh?"

"You were mumbling under your breath." She lifted a dubious eyebrow. "Assessing?"

"Not exactly." He tapped his temple. "Mental checklist. I may be a slob at home, but SAR is the real deal. Impacts lives. Sure, the other jobs pay the bills, but this one..." He stopped, unable to find the words.

"...fulfills a part of you?" she finished for him, somewhat emerging from her stupor much to his relief.

He squeezed her hand. "Exactly."

"What does Reka do?"

"She's an air-scent dog. The reason I had to stop at the fire station was to gather personal items so Reka can smell the scent. She works off lead for this, but she can do tracking or trailing on lead. Reka and I have this connection, we trust each other. She will go ahead, following the scent on the wind. I whistle, and she returns, and we continue that method until somebody is found." He reached and scratched Reka under the chin. "She's never let me down."

"And you?"

He tried to convey his competence with a smile. "I do what I'm trained for. I'm experienced in CPR and SOLO wilderness first aid emergency care. All those certs I told you about. We'll rely on Reka to help us, but I can look for tracks once we get beyond the shelter. We're hiking via a path they didn't use, opposite end. We'll start at Appalachian Gap. They came from the direction of Lincoln Peak. Also, snow will limit our access to footprints."

Ah, hell, this sounded bloody awful. Her sister—Surely, her mind was racing.

Charlotte adjusted her seat belt and stared at the road and trees. "Are there others like you? With dogs, I mean?"

"There are, but I'm the only dog handler in town right now. A few are being trained. The rest of the team members work without dogs, but there are other Vermont K9 units and handlers. Commander Bixler is calling everyone he can find. It sounds like he's not getting through to anyone. We're closest, and we have Reka. It's up to us."

"You can get in trouble bringing me."

"I'll tell you, this seems like an easier search. However..." He took a deep breath. "We won't know what we'll find...they could be hypothermic or disoriented. They must be fatigued to have been unable to hike down. We lost cell contact. Otherwise, we'd try to talk them down. There will be no cliff-climbing adventures like you see on TV, okay? Search, stabilize, signal the helo," he repeated from earlier.

"What happens when we reach the shelter?"

Okay, that was better. She was already planning to go with him.

"I'll radio and check in with Commander Bixler. We'll follow Reka's tracking from there. Most likely we'll continue on the Long Trail, but we'll keep to her guidance. Then we use flares to signal the helo after I call on the radio and activate a location beacon."

"I don't think I can do this."

That was better than outright refusal. "I won't force you. I do need another set of hands, and SAR volunteers never work solo. But I'll go alone if I must." Ouch, that sounded awful.

She licked her lips.

"You've got mad skills and keen first aid experience. Don't doubt yourself. You do all that training for the district, right?"

She nodded. "That's hypothetical. This is real."

He squeezed her knee. "Everything is hypothetical until it's real. You can do this."

Her knee trembled. "I haven't been on a mountain, a hill, since before..."

"I will be with you."

She turned to him, full trust in her eyes. "Okay. Let's go."

Twenty

With snowshoes tucked into her backpack, wind blasting her at the exposed trailhead, and fully outfitted in winter clothes, Charlotte evaluated the trail, her feet rooted to the spot. A harmless forest stood before her. Pine trees were reaching, beckoning her like an evil cartoon villain. Matiu crunched ahead in several inches of snow. Kids hiked this trail.

What if I fall? What if I fail?

What if one of us gets hurt? Or worse?

For crying out loud, Charlotte. Snap out of it!

This was not Chile. This was not a highly technical climb up soaring cliffs or 10,000-footers. This was a 4,000-foot mountain range in the pleasant Green Mountains. On a frigid April day hit by a freak snowstorm that had walloped the range with six inches of snow.

Like before.

She smacked the side of her head.

"Charlotte?"

"Huh?" Her other hand clung like glue to the page in the hiker's log. At least on this quiet, windy, chilly mountain,

they would not disappear or be forgotten. The commander knew Matiu's plan. Matiu had radioed him again. Still
no other crew to be roused. They were it.

She signed the log, too, with detailed information.
There had been no log or official check-in for Julie. Her
sister had left a message at one of the *refugios*, and *that
was it*. Gone off with some mysterious group. A morbid
thought in Charlotte's mind had always found its way to
the surface, that Julie had been abducted, assaulted, or
murdered.

No, she chided. Hiking accident.

Matiu approached. "They're not listed in there. I
looked. They came from the other end, like I said. We'll
strap the snowshoes on. Let's get our A into G. Time is of
the essence."

"Our what?"

He tilted his face. "You don't know that one?"

She summoned a half grin. He was trying. "Got it. My
ass is moving into gear. But 'honest to G' was *to God*. Now
you have me confused, Matiu." Wow, that was her stab at
humor. Well, sticky situations called for letting her brain
go. Letting pain and worry release.

The snowshoes were a struggle at first on the incline,
but each step got less cumbersome as she fell into a
groove. Matiu, natural tour guide, babbled on in his sexy,
conversant voice.

"...They began at Lincoln Gap. It's an eleven-mile, sev-
en-hour trip each way. But the road at Lincoln Gap is
closed in winter. That adds another four miles to their
hike. You can tackle four summits on the ridge, all in
the four-thousand range: Abraham, Lincoln, Ellen, and
Stark—that's where we're heading. They'd mentioned be-

ing between the two shelters on Stark. I won't lie. The Gap-to-Gap section is more difficult, but coming in from this end is easier."

She broke in. "They couldn't make it to either shelter?" She kept voicing the same questions, as if his answer might change if she asked it differently.

He shrugged, ahead of her a few steps as they sloshed through the powdery snow over hardened mud. "I guess not."

"How did they get an SOS message out?"

"Text message to a friend in town, then the call was sent to dispatch. However, the hikers have been nonresponsive to texts since last night. They slept here on the mountain. I hope they found a way to make a shelter."

She shivered. Exposed, alone, and in that windy, cold storm. Moisture puffed before her. Reka scurried ahead, bounding in the snow. They weren't close to the search location yet. They had to make it to the clearing first. Nausea rippled nerves in her empty stomach. Tea was not the best breakfast for a demanding hike.

Matiu was right. It was a relatively easy trail, though her knees kept cracking. It had been far too long. The hike was eerie with the winter-spring surroundings. Bare, scraggly trees, mud, snow, and spruce and pine. On the trail, they were relatively protected from the bellowing winds. It still felt like death to her.

Which was nonsense. It was just April snow on a mountain. This was not Chile. This was not a search for Julie. She couldn't shake the déjà vu experience though.

She made mental notes of every turn. Her heart pounded from adrenaline and effort. The steepness faded an hour into the climb.

"We're getting close to the clearing."

She focused on placing one foot in front of the other. Each step a renewal. Each breath closer to her own summit.

For a chatty guy, Matiu was focused, quiet.

They reached the shelter and ski lift without a problem.

With a soul-quenching breath, she almost sobbed at the clearing. Strong wind gusts ripped into them, and she stumbled. "Here," Matiu said, taking her hand and leashing Reka. "Let's rest for a moment in the shelter."

A relief from the roaring winds, the inside of the newer shelter was a cozy welcome. "Drink water, and please eat, Charlotte. You look pale. There's a propane heater if we double back here. If the stranded hikers are movable."

She slid off her backpack with a groan and absorbed the sight below her, out the window, down the mountain to the ski village. It was an amazing view. That she missed.

She ate a granola bar and apple, hoping the food would stay down in her queasy stomach. Matiu didn't look so well himself. He rummaged through his pack, his skin paler than normal, a light sheen of perspiration on his skin.

He did a quick periphery search and returned. He used the handheld radio instead of his phone. "Commander Bixler?"

"Copy, Matiu. Progress?"

"We just got to the first shelter. Going to send Reka now. We'll signal with the flares when we reach them. I'll radio and activate the location beacon from that point for the helo."

When. Not if. Charlotte loved Matiu's optimism.

"Good luck. Check in again on this channel. Still calling for crews. No response. Out."

"Out."

He turned to Charlotte. "Let's do this."

They exited the protection of the shelter, and Matiu let Reka off the leash after having her smell the piece of clothing. She was off, ahead, bells on her vest jingling. Matiu plodded behind in the snowshoes. "Charlotte?"

She hesitated but joined him. Along the way, he left markers, dice-sized, brightly orange tacks that he punctured into the tree trunks.

"Why the markers?" she asked.

"It's a well-cleared trail, with colored blazes, but with snow and mud and our footprints, we leave markers for any crew if they come this way."

"Will the chopper land back in the clearing?"

He shook his head. "They won't land. We'll radio them from the drop location. They will attempt to lower the crew as close as possible to the hikers."

"In the trees?"

"Or on the ridge, depending on where we find them. It's routine. They're trained for this. Easier than us two carrying a loaded stretcher down in this mess. Remember, we need four sets of hands to carry a stretcher out."

She remembered. But the idea of a helicopter lowering a Stokes stretcher, here, on the ridge, baffled her. "Okay." This didn't make her feel better.

"Plus, markers are used in case we go off path," he added.

That was worse. She quieted the nagging inner voice. This was not time to panic, to let fears rise to the surface.

Oh, but they bubbled anyway, like a pot set to boil on a burner, and left unattended. Splatters, pops, hisses.

A flash of yellow crossed her vision. There, a hazy movement in the trees. She saw it again. Bright yellow that stood out among the brown tree trunks and shadows. She paused and almost asked Matiu if he'd seen it. She blinked. No, it was gone. Her mind was playing tricks on her.

After a few minutes, he asked, "What do you want to see in New Zealand?"

She liked distraction. "Why?"

He slid his hand in hers, as was becoming habit.

Although both were gloved, his heat pulsed into her palm. "For me to plan for us...for when you come to see me."

Her hope faded. He was still going. Why would he stay for her? How could she expect him to drop his dream after knowing her for only a week? She wouldn't want that, either. But the fact that he *wanted* her to come warmed her soul.

She did the opposite of her usual coping mechanism of shutting down. She talked. And talked. She shared all the places on her wish list. Matiu seemed to be delighted with her enthusiasm. "I've been to all those places. I'll take you."

"This was just a—" she began.

"No, it wasn't."

He whistled. Reka returned, got a treat, smelled the clothing again, and was ahead of them, darting on and off the path in some sort of planned, but irregular method. She zigzagged between bushes and trees. Charlotte trusted this search method. This continued for another half hour.

Then, Matiu suddenly grabbed Charlotte's elbow. He had slowed down incredibly. "Wait, look."

Fresh tracks. That veered off the path. Reka was already off the path, ahead, following the tracks. "Why would they leave the trail?" she voiced. Reka's dark tail disappeared into the brown, knotty branches and thick evergreens.

"Injured. Disoriented. Dehydrated. Hypothermic." He paused, rested against a tree, and sneezed. He gripped his side with a moan.

"Matiu, what is it?"

"I'm knackered."

"What does that mean?"

"Dizzy, shaky. Are *you* okay?"

"I feel fine." She removed her glove and felt his forehead. He was sweating, which she thought had been from their efforts of snowshoeing, but his face was not flushed from exertion. It was pallid. "You never got the flu shot?" It was more of a statement than a question, as she knew the answer already.

He shook his head. "Let's go."

"You can't. You shouldn't have come up here."

"There was nobody else."

He exhaled a wheeze, followed by a gasp for breath.

"You mean you felt this way earlier? This morning and you didn't say?"

"Just thought—"

The wind tore across this part of the trail, numbing her ears. It was not safe for Matiu to carry on. Everything began to spin. Blood pounded in her head.

Reka returned, barking.

"She's found something...or them." He gave her a treat. "Good girl, Reka. Sweet girl." He shoved a bag of treats in Charlotte's hand. He located the flares. "Reka will guide you..." He began to shake uncontrollably.

Reka waited, face upturned to Charlotte. The dog sat, ready. She didn't pace or jump.

"What?" Charlotte asked.

He spoke in choppy sentences, his breathing strained. "I'll wait here. I'm dizzy, Charlotte. Here, the tree. On the trail. I'll stay here. You go with Reka. I'll radio the helo and trigger the location beacon, as we are close enough for them to get coordinates. Those folks need you. Cover them with the bivvy. Hydrate. Once you find them, signal with the LED flares. Set the smaller ones along the perimeter around where you locate them if there is a clearing."

He coughed, swallowed with a grimace, then took a few breaths. "Space them out as best you can. Get as high as you can, out of the tree line. Climb a boulder. If you can't stick them in the ground because of tree cover, which I suspect, given how dense the forest is here, you'll just need to wave the large one above your head. These LED flares are powerful, and though there are evergreens here, there are gaps in the deciduous trees. Not much foliage has filled in yet."

He pointed to the flares. "Those can be stuck in the ground or placed on a boulder, and one larger one you can hold. Can you do that?" He was already relocating gear between the two packs; she had brought her light-weight one.

She noted everything he said. "Are you kidding me?"

"Charlotte...repeat what I said," he said, firmly.

She inhaled, and did so, confidence shaking the worry from her. "Follow Reka. Give her treats if she returns. Stabilize the couple—food, water, bivvy. Signal the chopper crew with the flares. Wait."

"Yes."

She nodded, numb. Circulation left her fingertips, not from cold, but from terror. She needed to step off the path. Without Matiu. "What about you?"

"I'll be fine. Reka's got you. She will take you to them. Remember that Reka is trained to listen only to my orders. She knows to stay with them until help arrives unless I tell her otherwise. She will not return to me until everyone is safe and air lifted. I-I should come with you." He tried to stand upright and fell against the tree, heaving.

She shoved a water bottle in his hand. "Hydrate *yourself*. You need to rest. I promise to come back for you." She swiped a kiss on his cold cheek.

He coughed, nearly gagging on the water. "Get there and wait. The helo crew will lower a paramedic to secure the trampers. Then you and Reka can return to me."

"There's no trail..." Fear escalated to panic.

"Leave markers."

He handed them to her. "They have metal ends. Stick them in tree trunks."

She stood frozen in her spot for a long minute, all the while Matiu's words muted to the wind and her spinning mind. Reka sat patiently beside them. Markers, treats, helicopter, flares, stabilizing...

"Why can't we wait for another crew? There has to be more troopers."

"Time, Charlotte. Every minute adds to their exposure to elements. Nobody else is coming. We are so close. So close. You can help. The helo crew can handle this once they arrive."

She whimpered.

He grabbed her arms and gently shook her from her stupor. "You won't be lost to this mountain. The *maunga* will protect you."

She sniffled and nodded. "I can do this."

"Yes, yes, you can! You have Reka. You have me. We leave this mountain together, Charlotte." He coughed uncontrollably. Finally, he said, "Reka, Go! Go *slow*," he ordered. He gave Reka a treat.

Without time to refuse or fight, Charlotte was off on the dog's heels.

She got tangled in bushes as the burst of adrenaline faded and her snowshoes got caught on errant roots. Dammit! She inhaled pine and swiped the salty tears from her cheeks. "Julie, be with me. Help us." The wind screeched in response. Nearby trees groaned, some not well-rooted and moving with the gusts.

"Wait, Reka! Wait!" Damn that dog. Okay, she was just doing her job, but she went too fast, bobbing and weaving, barking. Charlotte struggled with the snowshoes off the trail, getting caught on roots and branches. She had to abort placing the markers. It was slowing her down. The dog might not circle back for her. Reka's bark grew distant and muffled.

There it was again, a flash of yellow. Like lemon yellow. A jacket. Was that them?

Reka's bark changed. It beckoned. From one spot. Charlotte followed the sound.

There were two people, a woman and man, huddled together against a rock in matching navy-blue parkas. "Good girl, Reka." She gave her another treat. "I'm here to help. I'm Charlotte."

"Tessa. And Rick. He's not well. He hasn't woken up today, and my ankle is twisted," the woman said. She was shivering, despite adequate layers.

Charlotte went to task, followed the instructions on the warming blanket, and got Rick into the thermal bivvy. She hoped it wasn't too much heat, but it was snowing. "You sure it's just a twist?"

Tessa bobbed her head. "I can walk on it a little bit. Doesn't feel broken."

Reka paced. Oh yes, flares. Charlotte placed the smaller ones around the area, highly doubting they'd be seen. She scrambled on top of two exposed boulders and placed flares on each. Thank God for glacial boulders in New England. She would turn on the bright handheld flare when she heard a chopper.

"Tell me what happened."

Tessa relayed their ordeal.

She had slipped when she thought she had heard or seen a bear. They had fallen off the trail and having thought they found it again, continued, but with the snow, got disoriented, taking them farther away on a false trail. The snowstorm had intensified overnight. Rick sent texts. Their batteries died.

Speaking of which. She pulled out her phone. Tried texting, then calling Matiu. Nothing. Well, hopefully he called the helicopter.

"Rest, rest. Help is coming. Let's get you warm and hydrated. Here's some food," Charlotte assured. She handed her a granola bar and banana.

"Rick wouldn't leave me. He tried once but then got lost and confused and found his way back."

He wasn't wearing as many layers as Tessa. Charlotte checked his warming blanket. It was working. Color was slowly returning to his face. She shook his shoulder. "Rick? Rick, can you hear me? I want you to drink some water." When he roused, she tipped the water bottle to his mouth.

She sat with them, close, shoulder to shoulder with Tessa. Both were younger, in their twenties. Rick swam in and out of consciousness, and Tessa tried to chat.

"When I saw you and your bright yellow coat, I thought I had seen an angel," Tessa said pushing a muddy swath of hair away from her forehead.

Charlotte's parka was red. Yellow?

"Ohhh...but it's not yellow. Must be seeing things," Tessa murmured.

Charlotte's stomach quivered. Perhaps Julie had been there in spirit, guiding her to these two. She wept inside. *Thank you, Jules. I love you.*

Reka sat so patiently. Charlotte gave her another treat.

Soon, a chopper roared in the distance. She turned on the handheld flare and climbed the boulder again, waving. The wind beat down upon her. It all happened in a whirlwind.

A chopper. Crewman. Lowering. Lifting.

The crewman moved fluidly through the motions of bringing Rick up to the chopper.

"Where's your team?" the man shouted over the roar above as he prepared to go up with Tessa.

"On the trail."

He nodded and was back up in the helicopter in no time.

Oh my God, they had done it. The couple would be okay.

Charlotte gathered her things. She needed to return to the trail and hike down with Matiu. The snowfall had grown heavier. Her path was buried beneath scraggly bushes and snow mushed with frozen mud. She couldn't see her tracks anymore, and Reka's pawprints were everywhere.

She rose. "Okay, Reka, we need to find Matiu. Go slow."

Reka bounded ahead. However, not being her handler, the dog didn't return to check in with Charlotte. The dog had accomplished her task. Minutes passed. Yeah. That's why she needed the markers. She shook the treats and called. Nope.

Charlotte took deep breaths and focused. She could do this. Her photographic memory was hard to explain. She located the "catalogued spot" she called it, inside her brain, of the trees, specific bushes, markings. It was like a snapshot every few feet.

She opened the photo album of her brain, accessed the memories, saw familiarities, and then chose which way to go. It was a flooding surge of memory. Before she knew it, she had reached her last marker, and there was Matiu, half awake and leaning against the same tree on the trail. Reka sat beside him. His eyes lit, a broadened smile stretching across his face.

She had done it.

Twenty-One

The next morning, Charlotte packed her belongings. Usually, everything had its place in plastic bags, assigned to designated corners of her suitcase or backpack. This time, she tossed her items in haphazardly.

Veronica and Josh were eating breakfast. She deposited her suitcase in the front hallway. Her mind still reeled with what had transpired in the past twenty-four hours.

The rescue on the mountain had been terrifying yet exhilarating. They saved Tessa and Rick. She still couldn't believe it. Courage had melted away her fears. And her heart felt a smidgen healed. Just a bit. The pain of loss still remained, but guilt and regret would no longer take a front seat in her brain.

Matiu helped her see that.

Matiu. He was resting, at home, as of last night with a prescription of chicken soup, ginger ale, and sleep. She wanted to visit him, say a proper goodbye, but it was too painful. Instead, she twiddled her thumbs until it was time to leave.

Tessa and Rick were at the hospital, recovering. All good, as Matiu would say.

She had not only summited the mountain, but she also made it down. Her body was achy in a rewarding way. She had missed this feeling.

She fell into the chair at the communal desk in the media center. Her phone started to ping with emails and messages, since the Wi-Fi was strongest near the wireless router.

To her surprise, she had an email from Esteban, her Chilean contact, timestamped with yesterday's date. She'd been so exhausted, so thrilled, so emotional after the rescue, she hadn't thought to check her email or gloom scroll on social media.

For once, *she hadn't thought about checking her email.*

"Oh my God." Her heart palpitated as she clicked his message with the subject "Update."

With one hand in her lap to control her knocking knees, she read and reread the email message twice, each time the words making more sense, each time a heartbreaking understanding.

Senorita MacGregor,

We finally located one of the hikers who had traveled with your sister, a Mr. Reynard Elvestad from Norway. It was hard to locate him, since your sister had not logged in with anyone besides leaving a brief message at the refugio. I'm sorry this has taken so long. I followed up on leads. We located her grave. My condolences are with you. The cemetery information is below. She and two others, who had not been identified until this Mr. Elvestad was located, are buried in an anonymous grave. Apparently, local

authorities had found them three weeks after the initial
search, but information was not properly conveyed to us.
I can proceed with exhuming but will require the official
documentation from your parents and the United States.
Below is the name of a representative Stateside, who can
be of assistance.

Mr. Elvestad spoke of her bravery in the storm. She chose
to stay with a stranded family who were awaiting rescue;
Mr. Elvestad trekked to find help. She tried to trek out after
no return from Mr. Elvestad. It is believed that she got
lost or was otherwise incapacitated. The parents in the
stranded family also perished, but their son was found alive
and recounted this story to us.

She died courageous, the ultimate sacrifice.

My apologies, senorita. May her soul and yours be at rest.
Esteban

Exhume? Her bones.

Charlotte's stomach churned. She abated her thoughts
and instead found comfort in Matiu's Māori story. Instead
of exhuming on the first anniversary of Julie's death, it
would be roughly five years. Her bones and her spirit
could finally be at rest, home in Massachusetts. Charlotte's own soul would find peace.

A part of her had always hoped to find Julie alive,
hidden away in some cottage in the jungle or shacking
with a local man. Julie would never have done that to her
family. Julie's soul might have been lost to the storm, but
Charlotte's...had returned yesterday.

She wept a new kind of tears. Closure.

Matiu could not stay in bed and be miserable. Charlotte was leaving today. It was already past nine in the morning. Lightheaded and feverish, he bundled himself in layers. He could not let her slip through his fingers.

It was crazy. For once, he wasn't aimless or restless. A vivid, clear sense of certainty fueled him. He had decided.

He parked on the street and stumbled to the kitchen entrance, trying to avoid touching things. He was probably highly contagious, so he had a bottle of hand sanitizer Charlotte left at his place, shoved in his pocket. He didn't have any spare masks kicking around.

His muscles ached with each step.

Charlotte had done it. She had saved that couple.

He coughed. *Ouch, scratchy throat.* He sure hoped Charlotte wouldn't get sick. Once recovered, he wanted heaps more of her. For as long as she'd have him.

Jared was exiting the kitchen with a trash bag, and he opened the door. "Hey, Matiu. I heard you were sick. Why are you here?"

Matiu glided in, hands free, keeping as far back from Jared as possible. "Just a quick visit."

"Nate's making a batch of his chicken soup. Looks like you need it."

Matiu nodded, but his brain felt like it rocked with the movement. "Did everyone check out for today?"

Jared's sparkling blue gaze darted to Nate, who was in the kitchen doing prep to assist staff, and back to Matiu.

"He knows. It's okay," Matiu assured.

"Not everyone. There's a group from Boston. Not sure where they went." He lowered his voice, "Maybe they like Tiana's gourmet coffees instead." He smirked. It was a running joke between Nate and Tiana about who had the better coffee.

Matiu nosed into the dining room anyway, then the media area. The stairs made him cower. His head spun, and his muscles throbbed. No way could he make it. He circled back to the kitchen to find Nate gone, but Jared was still buzzing about, looking for something.

"Matiu, you look like death."

"Feel it, too."

"Go home. Can I relay a message to her?"

Matiu's hand grew clammy around the twisted *pikorua* pendant.

His mum had said to give it to *the one*.

The one with whom he formed a strong bond, the one he would want a lifetime connection with...the one he loved.

Charlotte.

"Let me try another spot."

Unsteady, he made his way to the porch. Crisp, cold morning air hit his face as he walked out the front door.

There she was, huddling within a quilt on a chair. "Matiu!" She dropped the quilt from her shoulders and hurried to him. "You're sick. Why aren't you home in bed?" She held him upright, arms embracing his middle.

Courage drove him. He caressed her cheek. "A*ta mārie.*"

Her face brightened with his greeting. "It is a good morning."

He opened his hand to show her the necklace. "I wanted to give this to you before you left."

She looked down but didn't take it. Pain pinched his spirit.

She doesn't want me.

A healthy glow filled her cheeks. She wasn't the least bit sick. She tilted her chin up. He tried not to breathe on her. However, he had already done way more.

"You can't give me that," she said.

"I can, and I will."

Her bottom lip trembled. "I know its meaning, remember?"

"Exactly."

He opened her hand and placed the pendant in her palm. Now was the time to say it. "I won't go, Charlotte. I won't leave you." It took every breath to say the final offer. "I won't go to New Zealand." He needed to act his age. Settle down. Stop chasing dreams.

Her eyes widened. "No."

Her words crushed his heart and soul.

"You need to go, Matiu. It's your dream." She nibbled a lip, quivering in his arms.

He needed to kiss her. Damn germs. "My dreams are just that."

"They are more than that. You can't throw them away for me."

She was right. For the first time he wanted to plant his feet in one place—with Charlotte. "You'd be in your glory in Aotearoa, ya know? I don't want to go without you."

Her lashes swept over her eyes.

He wished he could smell her delicious scent through his clogged sinuses.

"My year is almost done," she said, turning wet eyes to him.

His brain wasn't firing quickly today.

"My school year," she clarified. "It's summer here in a few months and winter in New Zealand, but I'm sure I can find something to do while you set up your business." A tremulous smile broke the frown.

"You'll come?" He squeezed her tighter.

"Yes."

"Oh, I can show you awe-inspiring places. It's a land of magic, mystery, and a deep soul."

"Not as soulful as you."

She squeaked in his tight embrace. Then, she brushed a lock of his hair aside, ran her finger down his cheek, and stared longingly into his eyes.

"You were right," she said in a breathy whisper.

"About what?"

"That this—us—is *more*. Julie showed me that life is short. I need to embrace it and take a leap of faith."

He felt suddenly hyperaware of his body. The thudding of his heart. The feel of her within his arms. The jolt of energy was coursing through his middle, despite his fatigue. "This is so much more. You'll come, then? Really?" he repeated, as if his ears had played a trick on him.

He didn't ask for how long. They'd leave that to fate.

Though he hoped it would be forever.

"Yes." She sniffled and squeezed him tighter as she rested her cheek against his chest. "I can't wait."

EPILOGUE

As Matiu would say, late November in New Zealand was *choice*.

Charlotte didn't think her eyes could absorb more beauty after their trips to Lake Tekapo and the Ahuriri River last week. On that outing, she had to swap out her camera memory card again to make room for more photos after taking hundreds of snapshots of the stunning lupins set against the beauty of the Southern Alps.

Pinks, purples, whites. The sea of stalky flowers waved at them.

Julie would have loved this region of the South Island. Charlotte's eyes were on overload. Could a place be too beautiful?

Lake Pukaki was another jewel in the rough. The bright blue glacial waters, with Aoraki's majestic peak in the distance...was just breathtaking.

And the night skies? Wow, just wow. In the middle of July, while Matiu had taken a group on a night skies tour, during the cold months of winter, he lugged along his hundred-pound telescope, Dob, and stargazed while

Charlotte took night photos. They saw the galactic core of the Milky Way at its brightest, the Southern Cross, and Magellanic Clouds. Science and the soul threaded together all in one blissful moment.

Later, she sat, wrapped in a warm blanket and in the comfort of Matiu's arms, safe, loved. She took in the silent beauty of it all and felt peace wash over her. Julie was with her.

Matiu was at home here in Aotearoa. He maneuvered on trails as if he'd walked them his entire life. It didn't matter if they were new or unfamiliar to him. Each adventure was a renewal: a trek on the volcanic Tongariro Crossing, a drive through Arthur's Pass in the snowy Southern Alps, a stroll around thermal hot springs, a walk upon the golden shores of Abel Tasman, ventures across floating swing bridges, and a ferry ride through Marlborough Sounds from the North Island...

Food, culture, people, wildlife, excursions.

So many marvels had been checked off her bucket list.

But it wasn't a list anymore. It was life.

Charlotte was stretching her legs and feeding her soul in the wild wonders with Matiu at her side.

He had brought her to New Zealand to explore...and to remember.

And remember she did.

Now, on this glorious November day, she thumbed the *pikorua* necklace resting flat against her chest. A pleasant warmth hummed from the jade, like a kiss against her heart. Today it was just them, no guided tour group, though Matiu's planner was bursting with bookings.

They were halfway through the hair-raising twenty-mile drive that made the windshield rattle and Jeep vibrate over a rustic gravel road. Charlotte focused on settling her pulse with deep breaths. With every bump and rut, she took in the lush, green Matukituki Valley.

A few times, she had suggested turning right around, afraid the front windshield would shatter.

Sheep and cattle glared at them as they noisily rumbled down the road.

"Well, I certainly feel inspired," she said, tongue-in-cheek. They were on their way to the Rob Roy Trek near Mount Aspiring, which the Māori called Tititea.

Matiu loosened his hands on the steering wheel and wiped sweat off his brow. "Remember how much you like water?" he asked, his face all dimples.

Could he be any cuter? He was in his glory.

She lifted her eyebrow dubiously. Much like he had shown her the water wonders in Vermont—their kayak on the Mad River and the waterfall climb where he first kissed her—he had done the same here. They had paddled majestic Milford Sound and saw countless waterfalls bursting from the spring thaw.

"Our glacier tour is next week, isn't it?" she asked, trying to sip from her water bottle as they bumped along. She splashed her shirt and gave up. She couldn't wait for their heli hike on Fox Glacier.

"Well, we have one more water adventure first." His dark brown eyes sparkled.

Ahead, Charlotte saw the most unusual road sign. A black exclamation point set on a yellow diamond-shaped background, the word "FORD" written beneath.

"Wha-"

Her words must have fallen out of her brain on the jolting drive here.

"Remember? You love water." He laughed lightly.

"And mountains again, too," she said with a squeeze of his knee. "Thanks to you."

"Well, today you get both. Just a ford across the river. The Jeep can handle it. Need you to guide me a bit, so we don't hit a big boulder and puncture a tire."

"No pressure," she tittered.

He stopped the vehicle in front of the river crossing. It looked both terrifying and exciting. Just about twenty feet across, maybe a few feet deep. At least the Jeep had good clearance, and water wouldn't go up the tailpipe. She bit her lip and nodded.

She gripped the door, steeling herself while glancing at the simple diamond adorning her left ring finger.

And in they went, slowly, but surely. Maybe the bumpy road and the river crossing were a way for New Zealanders to keep the non-serious tourists away. The former Charlotte would have turned right around at this point.

Her heart pounded, her mind buzzed. She found herself rising in her seat, mentally lifting the vehicle. The Jeep nosed down in and she guided him across the slowly moving river. Water splashed the windshield. The scent of freshness through the open windows filled the car. Her stomach was a riot of butterflies as her body rolled with the maneuver, a bit to the right, then to the left. He went slow, and she heard every turn of the wheel. The tires crunched on the riverbed, and then up, up, up they came out.

They both breathed an audible sigh as they emerged. "Exhilarating!" she said.

Matiu whooped.

He drove onward. "Glad you feel that way, because, uh, we have six more of these to cross before the trailhead."

She playfully punched his shoulder and laughed, because she knew he was serious.

"Ready?" he asked as they approached the next river crossing.

She returned his smile, just as big, just as bright, her words full of trust. "Let's do this."

Acknowledgments and Author's Note

With gratitude, I thank everyone who took the time to answer all my questions or read through a manuscript draft for authenticity and accuracy. Be it help with Vermont Search and Rescue procedures including the canine unit, Vermont State Police policies, New Zealand, Māori culture, vernacular, or the perspective of my unique characters, thank you all for helping me bring this story to life. Thank you to my amazing support team of authors, Lorraine and Janet. Thank you to Angela Westerman for another gorgeous cover.

Have I been to the Mad River Valley of Vermont? Yes, lots of times. My first trip was to do research for Soul of the Storm, actually, about eight years ago. Since then, I've been all over Vermont many times in summer and winter (my family loves to mountain bike and ski). What about New Zealand? Oh my, yes. And it is one of my favorite places in the world. I hope my story did this beautiful country justice. Thank you as always, for reading!

ABOUT THE AUTHOR

Jean has a penchant for the misunderstood, be it sharks, microbes, or wounded characters. A scientist by training, she now spends her days as an author and champion for her children. She draws from her interest in history, science, the outdoors, and her family for inspiration. She serves on the local library board of trustees and is an advocate for community, inclusion, and diversity.

A nature enthusiast who adores the national parks, Jean also writes for family-oriented travel magazines and websites. When not writing, she enjoys gardening, tackling the biggest mountains in New England, and going on adventures with her husband and children, while taking snapshots of the world around her and daydreaming about the next story.

Find out more about her books by visiting her website: www.jeanmgrant.com